"Did you let your father know that you're looking for Sarah?"

A muscle worked in Carson's jaw and he shifted. "I did."

"And?" she prompted, sipping her coffee.

"He was a little too touched," Carson said. "Even though I made it clear I'm not doing this to find his supposed second great love. I'm doing it to prove that he'll feel absolutely nothing for this woman so he can go back to living his life."

"What if he *does* feel something?" Olivia asked. "Yes, I know, power of suggestion, blah, blah, blah. But you can't fake chemistry, a pull toward someone, a quickening of your pulse, an inexplicable draw."

She knew because she felt it with Carson. She couldn't stop stealing peeks at him—the strong profile, the broad shoulders, the muscular thighs.

"It would be pretty random for my father to meet some stranger and fall instantly in love. I have no doubt he'll feel toward Sarah Mack the way he feels when he meets anyone. The earth won't move."

"What if it does?" she asked.

He looked at her, clearly frustrated. "It won't."

She couldn't help a chuckle. "You sure are set in your ways."

"You are, too."

"Nope," she said. "I'm open to possibility."

HURLEY'S HOMESTYLE KITCHEN:
There's nothing more delicious than falling in love...

Dear Reader,

When I was thirty years old, my mom and I were on vacation in New Orleans, and as we were walking around the beautiful French Quarter, a young man with long, wild hair and old-soul dark eyes approached us, a card hanging from his neck that read Palm Readings—$5.00. I handed over the five bucks and he said, "Whatever you're doing, you should be doing the opposite. If you're an actress, you should be a director. If you're a teacher, you should be a student." Okay, his reading could have meant something to anyone, but what he said had a big impact on me. I was a book editor at the time, and the opposite was my longtime dream that I'd shied away from. I went back home and scarily did flip what I was doing. Four years later, I sold my first novel to Harlequin.

Did my palm reader have special abilities? Was he just a good reader of faces, of hopes and dreams? I've always wanted to explore that very question, so I handed it over to my characters: Olivia, a food-truck cook who *does* have special abilities—she can restore hope through her cooking—and Carson, a pragmatic private investigator and single father who only believes in cold, hard reality. Olivia's late mother was a fortune-teller whose final client was Carson's father, a man who deeply wants to believe in his romantic fortune. And so a prediction ends up changing the lives of several characters in the small town of Blue Gulch, Texas.

I hope you enjoy Olivia and Carson's story, and I would love to hear from you. Did you know that Meg Maxwell is a pen name? My real name is Melissa Senate. You can write to me at AuthorMegMaxwell@gmail.com or at MelissaSenate@yahoo.com.

All my best,

Meg Maxwell

The Cook's
Secret Ingredient

———

Meg Maxwell

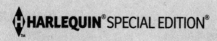
HARLEQUIN® SPECIAL EDITION®

Recycling programs
for this product may
not exist in your area.

ISBN-13: 978-0-373-62329-7

The Cook's Secret Ingredient

Printed in U.S.A.

Meg Maxwell lives on the coast of Maine with her teenage son, their beagle and their black-and-white cat. When she's not writing, Meg is either reading, at the movies or thinking up new story ideas on her favorite little beach (even in winter) just minutes from her house. Interesting fact: Meg Maxwell is a pseudonym for author Melissa Senate, whose women's fiction titles have been published in over twenty-five countries.

Books by Meg Maxwell

Harlequin Special Edition

Hurley's Homestyle Kitchen

A Cowboy in the Kitchen
The Detective's 8 lb, 10 oz Surprise
The Cowboy's Big Family Tree

In dear memory of Gregory Pope.

Chapter One

Olivia Mack added a generous sprinkle of powdered sugar to the chocolate-dipped cannoli and then handed it through Hurley's Homestyle Kitchen's food-truck window to the waiting customer. Would the confection work its magic? Of course it would. Olivia's food—from blueberry pancakes to fried chicken to lemon chiffon pie—had been lifting spirits for as long as Olivia had been cooking, which was since girlhood. According to her mother, Olivia had a gift. Supposedly her food changed moods, healed hearts, restored hope.

Come on. Olivia hardly believed that. Comfort food comforted; it was right there in the name. If you were feeling down, a plate of macaroni and cheese did its job. And a chocolate-dipped cannoli with a sprinkling of powdered sugar? How could it not bring about a smile? Nothing magic about that.

Sorry if you don't like it, but you have a gift, same as I do, same as all the women on my side of the family, her mother had always said. Miranda Mack passed away just over a month ago, and Olivia still couldn't believe her larger-than-life mother was gone.

"Did you add chocolate chips to one end and crushed pistachios to the other like I asked?" Penny Jergen snapped from the other side of the food-truck window as she inspected the cannoli, her expression holding warring emotions. Olivia could see anger, pain, humiliation and plenty of heartbreak in Penny's green eyes.

Which had Olivia refraining from rolling her own eyes at Penny's usual rudeness. "Sure did." *As you can clearly see.*

Barely mustering a thank-you, Penny carried the cannoli in its serving wedge over to the wrought iron tables and chairs dotting the town green just steps from the food truck. Olivia watched Penny stare down the young couple at the next table who were darting glances at her, then sit, her shoulders slumping. Olivia felt for Penny. The snooty twenty-six-year-old local beauty pageant champ wasn't exactly the nicest person in Blue Gulch, but Olivia knew what heartbreak felt like.

Everyone in town had heard through the grapevine that Penny had caught her brand-new fiancé of just one week in bed with her frenemy, who'd apparently wanted to prove she could tempt the guy away from Miss Blue Gulch County. Ever since, Penny had walked around town on the verge of tears, head cast down. A barista at the coffee shop, Penny had handed Olivia her iced mocha that morning with red-rimmed eyes, her usually meticulously made-up face bare and crumpling. Olivia had been hoping Penny would stop by the food truck so Olivia could help a little. This afternoon she had.

As Olivia worked on a pulled-pork po'boy with barbecue sauce for her next customer, a young man with a nervous energy, as though he was waiting for news of some kind, she eyed Penny through the truck's front window. Penny bit into the cannoli, a satisfied *ah* emanating from her. She took another bite. As expected, Penny sat up straighter. She took another bite and her teary eyes brightened. Color came back to her cheeks. She slowly ate the rest of the cannoli, sipped from a bottle of water, then stood up, head held high, chin up in the air.

"You know what?" Penny announced to no one in particular, flipping her long blond beachy waves behind her shoulders. "Screw him! I'm Penny Jergen. I mean, look at me." She ran her hand down her tall, willowy, big-chested frame. "That's it. Penny Jergen is done moping around over some cheating jerk who didn't deserve her." With that she left her balled-up, chocolate-dotted napkin on the table and marched off in her high-heeled sandals.

Olivia smiled. Penny Jergen, like her or not, was back to her old self. Presto-chango—whether Olivia liked her ability or not. The moment Penny had ordered the cannoli, chocolate chips on one end, crushed pistachios on the other, Olivia had instinctively known the extra ingredient the dessert had needed: a dash of "I'm Gonna Wash That Man Right Outa My Hair." A person couldn't get over heartbreak so fast—Olivia knew that from personal experience. But Olivia's customers' moods and facial expressions and stories told her what they needed and that telling infused the ingredients of their orders with…not magic, exactly, but something Olivia couldn't explain.

Her mother used to argue with her over the word *magic* all the time, going on and on about how there *was* magic in the world, miracles that couldn't be explained away, and Olivia would be stumped. All she knew for sure was that she believed in paying attention: watching faces, reading moods, giving a hoot. If you really looked at someone, you could tell so much about them and what they needed. And so Olivia put all her hopes for the person in her food and the power of positive thinking did its thing.

This was how Olivia tried to rationalize it, anyway. Special abilities, gifts, whatever you wanted to call it—she just wasn't sure she believed in that. Even if sometimes she stayed up late at night, trying to explain to herself her mother's obvious ability to predict the future. Olivia's obvious ability to restore through her food. It was one thing for Olivia to fill a chocolate cannoli shell with cream and sprinkle it with powdered sugar while thinking positively about female empowerment and getting over a rotten fiancé. It was another for those thoughts to actually have such a specific effect on the person eating that cannoli.

You have a gift, Olivia's mother had repeated the day she passed away. *My hope is that one day you'll accept it. Don't deny who you are. Denial is why—*

Her mom had stopped talking then, turning away with a sigh. Olivia knew she'd been thinking about her sister, Olivia's aunt, who'd estranged herself from Miranda and Olivia five years earlier. If her aunt had a gift, Olivia had never heard mention of it.

She forced thoughts of her family from her mind; she couldn't risk infusing her current customer's order with her own worries. She had to focus on him. She turned around and glanced at the guy, early twenties, biting his lower lip. He was waiting for a job offer, Olivia thought. Her fingers filling with good-luck vibes, she added the delicious-smelling barbecue sauce to his pulled-pork po'boy, wrapped it up and handed it to him through the window. She loved knowing that in about fifteen minutes, he'd have a little boost of confidence—whether or not he got the job.

And she wasn't in denial of who she was. Gift or no gift, Olivia knew exactly who she was: twenty-six, single and struggling to find her place now that her world had shifted. Until a week ago she'd been a caterer and personal chef, making Weight Watchers points-friendly meals for a few clients, gluten-free dishes for two other clients, and creating replicas of favorites that Mr. Crenshaw's late wife used to cook for him. She would never quit on her clients; she knew the effect her food had on them, but spending so much time alone in the kitchen of her tiny house, after having her heart broken and losing her mother, she'd needed *something*, something new, something that would get her outside and interacting with people instead of just with her stove.

And then Essie Hurley, who owned the popular restaurant Hurley's Homestyle Kitchen, had called, asking if Olivia, who she often hired to help out in the kitchen for big events, had any interest in running Hurley's Homestyle Kitchen's new business venture—the food truck. Olivia hadn't hesitated. Two other cooks at Hurley's would split the shifts, so Olivia was on three days a week from 11:30 a.m. to 3:30 p.m., and two days from

3:30 p.m. to 7:30 p.m. That left lots of time for her to cook at home for her clients and make her deliveries. The Hurley's Homestyle Kitchen food truck was parked several blocks down from the restaurant and business was bustling, the residents of Blue Gulch coming back time and again. Because—if she said so herself—she was a good cook. She really would like to think that was all there was to it. Good food, comforting food, delicious food, made people happy. End of story.

Olivia glanced out the window, grateful there was no one waiting and that she could take a break and have a po'boy herself. She was deciding between roast beef and grilled chicken when she realized that the stranger who'd been standing across the sidewalk in front of the coffee shop was still there, still watching her. At first she'd thought he was reading the chalkboard of menu items hanging from the outside of the food truck. But for twenty minutes?

And he didn't look particularly happy. Every time she caught his eye, which was every time she looked at him, he seemed to be glaring at her. But why? Who was he? Blue Gulch was a small town and if a six-two, very attractive man had moved in, Olivia would have heard about it from the grapevine. People chatted at the food-truck window as they passed the time until their orders were ready. Sometimes they talked out loud to her, sometimes she just heard snippets of conversation.

Olivia couldn't remember ever seeing the guy before. He stood to the side of the door of Blue Gulch Coffee in his dark brown leather jacket and jeans and cowboy boots, his thick brown hair lit by the sun, a large cup of coffee in his hand.

Just as she decided on grilled chicken with pesto-dill sauce, he walked up to the food truck. Whoa, he was good-looking. All that wavy chestnut-brown hair, green-hazel eyes, a strong nose and jawline and one dimple in his left cheek that softened up his serious expression a bit. Late twenties, she thought, unable to stop staring.

"May I help you?" Olivia asked, her Spidey senses going on red alert. This guy was seriously pissed off at something—and that something was her. Could you be angry at someone you'd never met? She tried to read him, to feel something, but her usual ability failed her.

He glared at her. "I'll have a sautéed-shrimp po'boy. Please."

She could tell that he'd struggled to add the *please*. "Coming right up."

He waited a beat, his eyes narrowed, then he glanced inside the truck, clearly trying to look around. For what?

She got to work, adding the shrimp, coated with her homemade Cajun seasoning, into the frying pan, and realized she was getting absolutely nothing from him. No vibe, other than his anger. But suddenly, a feeling came over Olivia, a feeling she usually didn't have to think so hard about. He was worried about someone, she realized. She had no idea who or why or what. She only knew the anger was masking worry.

She dared a peek at him. He stood to the side of the window, staring at her, his expression unchanged. *Is he worried about a relative?* The thought flitted out of her head as quickly as it had come in. She wasn't psychic. She couldn't read minds. But sometimes a thought would drift inside her like smoke, sometimes so fleetingly she couldn't grasp it.

She slathered each side of the French roll with the rémoulade of mustard and mayonnaise and horseradish sauce, then layered the sautéed shrimp and added tomato slices and onion. She could feel "it'll be okay" sparking from her fingers, infusing the po'boy.

She handed him the yellow cardboard tray holding his sandwich. He nodded and thanked her, then moved a few feet over to a pub table that lined the edge of the grass.

He shot another glare her way, then glanced left and right, up and down Blue Gulch Street. Was he waiting for someone? Watching for something? He'd been eyeing the truck for at least twenty minutes. He took a bite of the po'boy and she could tell, at least, that he liked the sandwich. He took another bite. No change in his expression. Then another. Still no change.

He appeared at the window. Same expression. Same glare.

The sautéed-shrimp po'boy hadn't worked on him. According to the man's face, it most certainly was not going to be okay.

Huh. That was weird. And a first, really.

"Are you the daughter of Miranda Mack?" he asked.

She stiffened. "Yes," she said, wondering what this was about.

He looked around the inside of the narrow truck before his hazel eyes settled back on her. "So you just serve po'boys and cannoli out of the truck? Not fortunes, too?"

Did he want his fortune told? Olivia didn't get that sense from him at all. "I'm not a fortune-teller. Just a cook."

He stared at her. "Look, I'd appreciate it if you could settle a family problem your mother caused."

Uh-oh. She'd been here a time or two or three or four over the years. Sometimes her mother's predictions upset her clients or their families, and when pleading with Miranda hadn't helped, they'd come to Olivia, asking her to intervene, hoping she could convince her mother to change the fortune or "see" something else.

He stepped closer. "Your mother told my father a bunch of nonsense about the second great love of his life, and now he's traveling all over Texas to find this woman. I'd appreciate it if you could put an end to this…ridiculousness."

Oh, boy.

"Mr.…" she began, stalling.

"My name is Carson Ford."

Olivia knew that name. Well, not Carson, but Ford. Her mother had mentioned a Ford. Edward or something like that.

"My father is Edmund Ford," he said, lowering his voice. "Suffice it to say he's a bigwig at Texas Trust here in Blue Gulch. He's also a vulnerable widower. Your mother told him that his second great love is a hairstylist named Sarah with green eyes. He's now racing around to every hair salon in the county asking for Sarahs with green eyes. People are going to think he's nuts. He's had seven haircuts in the past two weeks."

Oliva froze. Hair salon. Sarah. Green eyes. That could only be one person.

He narrowed his eyes at her. "She filled you in on this scam?"

Olivia bit her lip. Her aunt, her mother's sister who'd

gotten into a terrible argument with Miranda five years ago and hadn't been seen or heard from since, was named Sarah. And a hairstylist. With green eyes.

What the heck was this? *Oh, Mom, what did you do?*

He waited for her to respond, but when she didn't, he said, "Look, will you please talk some sense into my father? Explain that your mother ran a good game, a scam, fed people what they wanted to hear for lots of money. My father can go back to his normal life and I can focus on my own. This is interfering with my job and people are counting on me."

She felt herself bristle at the word *scam*, but she ignored it. For now. "What is your job?" She hadn't meant to ask that, but it came tumbling out of her mouth.

"I'm a private investigator. I specialize in finding people who don't want to be found—mostly of the criminal and/or fraudulent variety," he added with emphasis.

She stepped back, not expecting that. She didn't know what she'd expected him to say he did for a living, but private investigator wasn't it. Actually, she'd been thinking lawyer. Shark, at that.

She herself had thought about hiring a private investigator to find her aunt when her own online searches had led nowhere. Suffice it to say, to use his own phrase, that Carson Ford would not be interested in helping to locate this particular Sarah. "My mother is not a criminal or a fraud." *And she's gone*, she thought, her heart pinching.

He didn't respond. He just continued to stare at her as if waiting for her to give something away with her expression, catch her in a lie. This man clearly also paid attention to people; it was his job to do so. She would have to be careful around him.

Wait a minute. No, she did not. Her mother's business was her mother's business. Olivia had no secrets, nothing to hide about Miranda Mack.

Her mother's face, her dark hair wound into an elegant topknot affixed with two rhinestone-dotted sticks, her fair complexion, her long, elegant nose, her penchant for iridescent silver jewelry and long filmy scarves all came to mind. Olivia ached for the sight of Miranda. What she would give for one more day with her mother, another hug.

Despite their differences, Olivia missed her mother so much that tears crept up on her constantly. In the middle of the night. When she was brushing her teeth. While she was making her mother's favorite meal, pasta carbonara with its cream and pancetta, the only thing that could comfort Olivia lately when grief seized her. And guilt. For how Olivia had always dismissed her mother's surety that Olivia had a gift. Or that Miranda, the most sought-after fortune-teller in town—in the county—had had a gift, either. A crystal ball and some floaty scarves and deep red lipstick and suddenly her mother turned into Madam Miranda behind garnet velvet curtains. People liked the shtick, her mother had insisted. Olivia would say that three quarters of the town's residents believed that Miranda had been the real deal. A quarter had rolled their eyes. Olivia was mostly in the latter camp with a pinkie toe in the former. How to make sense of all her mother's predictions coming true?

Like the one about Olivia's own broken heart. A proposal that would never come from her long-term boyfriend. *He's not the one*, Miranda had insisted time and again, shaking her head.

"My mother passed away six weeks ago," Olivia said, her own blindness, her losses and this man's criticism all ganging up on her. "I won't stand for you to disparage her."

His expression softened. "I did hear about her death. I am very sorry for your loss."

She could tell that part was sincere, at least.

And she'd been right, she thought as she glanced at him. He was worried about a relative. His father.

He cleared his throat. "My father is expecting me for dinner tonight at his house. If you could come and talk some sense into him, I'd appreciate it."

What? No. No. No. He was inviting her to dinner at his father's house? To talk the man out of looking for this second great love? Who, according to Miranda, was very likely Olivia's aunt.

A woman her mother had been estranged from for five years. Had her mother "known" that this prediction would lead the man's son, a private investigator, to get huffy and intervene? That it would bring Sarah Mack home? *If* it brought Aunt Sarah home.

Olivia had never known her mother to do anything for her own gain. Never. If Miranda had told Edmund Ford that his second true love was a hairstylist named Sarah with green eyes, then her mother absolutely believed that to be true. Aunt Sarah or no Aunt Sarah.

"I—I…" She had no idea how to get out of this, or what she could possibly say anything to his father about his fortune. "My mother believed in her gift. Her fortunes came true eighty-five percent of the time."

He rolled his eyes. "Yes, I know all about the power of suggestion."

So did Olivia. And she also knew how badly her mother wanted Olivia to find Aunt Sarah. On the day of her death, Miranda had told Olivia she'd written a letter to her sister and that it was her dying wish that Olivia give it to Sarah along with a family heirloom, a bracelet passed down from their mother. Over the past six weeks, Olivia had tried to find Sarah by doing internet searches, but all her leads were for the wrong Sarah Mack. She'd even searched for Sarah Macks in hair salons in the surrounding counties and had come up empty, too. No wonder Edmund Ford hadn't been able to find her. No one could.

Maybe she should tell Carson Ford he didn't have to worry, that it was doubtful his father would ever find his "second great love."

"I'm surprised your father hasn't asked you to find her," Olivia said, wiping down the window counter. "I mean, there must be hundreds of green-eyed hairstylists named Sarah in the state of Texas. No last name, nothing else to go on?" she asked, fishing. It was possible that Edmund Ford's second great love wasn't Sarah Mack. There likely *were* hundreds of green-eyed hairstylists named Sarah in Texas.

He stepped closer to the window, bracing his hands on the sides of the wooden counter. "First of all, my father did ask me to help. But come on. How would trying to find this woman actually *help* my father? It's a wild-goose chase and nonsense. Second of all—" He stopped, as if realizing he was about to disclose personal family business to a stranger. He cleared his throat again. "There was one more thing," he added.

"My father asked your mother how he'd know for sure which green-eyed hairstylist named Sarah was his predicted love. Your mother said he would know her instantly, but that she would have a small tattoo of a hairbrush and blow-dryer on her ankle."

So much for the possibility that Miranda hadn't been talking about Sarah Mack. Olivia was twelve when her aunt had gotten that tattoo. The brush was silver and the blow-dryer hot pink, Aunt Sarah's favorite color.

"I'm not sure what I could possibly do or say to help you, Carson. I'm not a fortune-teller. I don't know how my mother's ability worked. If she said that his great love was this green-eyed tattooed hairstylist named Sarah, then she truly believed it. And like I said, her predictions were right most of the time."

He grimaced. "Oh, please. I don't believe that. I don't believe any of it."

Olivia didn't want to, either. But evidence was walking around all over town in the form of couples her mother had brought together or people who'd changed their lives because of what Miranda had predicted. "She was responsible for over three hundred marriages. She directed people to their passions, stopped them from making mistakes. Sometimes they listened, sometimes the heart wants what it wants even when a fortune-teller says it won't happen."

He scowled, then pulled out a checkbook from an inside pocket. "I'll pay you for your time. One hour, two tops, for you to talk some sense into my father. Five thousand ought to do it."

Five thousand dollars. Man, she could use that money. And she felt for Carson, she really did. "It's not about the money, Carson. It wasn't for my mother, either. I know that's hard for you to believe, but it's true."

He put away the checkbook. He tilted his head back, frustration and worry etched on his handsome face. She could feel it all over him, swirling in the air between them. "Please," he said. "My father hasn't been the same since my mother died five years ago. He's so… vulnerable. I know he's terribly lonely. I don't know what made him seek out your mother—*if* he sought out your mother—"

"My mom didn't lure clients to her," Olivia said gently. "She didn't need to. She had an excellent reputation. People came to her."

He scowled. "Edmund Ford would not go walking into some fortune-teller's little velvet-curtained room. He must have been led by something or fed some lies. Your mother ensnared him and then filled his head with nonsense. I can only imagine how much he paid her. My father, as I'm sure you know, is a very wealthy man. Making fraudulent claims, taking money from vulnerable people—that is against the law."

Anger boiled in Olivia's belly. "My mother was not a criminal! How dare you imply—"

"Dada!"

Olivia stuck her head farther out the window at the sound of the little voice. She watched a toddler, no older than two, run to Carson, who kneeled down, his arms wide, a big smile suddenly on the man's face. All traces of his anger were gone.

He wrapped the child in his arms and scooped him up. The little boy pointed at a picture on the food truck's menu, probably one of the cannoli.

"I have cookies for you at home," Carson said, giving him a kiss on his cheek.

A woman in her fifties, who Olivia recognized from around town, approached wheeling a stroller, and Carson smiled at her. "I'll take him from here," he told her. "Thanks for taking such good care of him, as always."

"My pleasure, Carson," she said. "I'm happy to babysit for as long as you're in town. See you tomorrow, sweetie," she added to the little boy, ruffling his hair before turning to walk away.

"Bye!" the boy called and waved.

"Your son?" Olivia asked, noting that Carson wasn't wearing a wedding ring. She smiled at the adorable child. "He looks just like you."

He nodded. "He's eighteen months old. Daniel is his name. Danny for short."

She wondered where Danny's mother was. Was Carson divorced? Widowed? Never married the little one's mother? It was possible. Olivia's mother hadn't married Olivia's father or anyone else. Her aunt Sarah had never married. Now Olivia was following in the family tradition.

Danny tilted his head, his big hazel eyes on his father. "Chih-chih tates?"

Carson smiled and pulled an insulated snack bag from the stroller basket. He unzipped it and handed the boy a cheddar cheese stick. "How about some cheese for now and then yes, in just a couple of hours we'll be going to Granddaddy's house for your favorite— roast chicken and potatoes with gravy." He glanced at Olivia. "*Chih-chih tates* is toddler speak for *chicken and potatoes*."

Danny grinned and munched his cheese stick. The

boy was so cute that Olivia wanted to sweetly pinch his big cheeks.

Carson put the snack bag away and shifted the toddler in his arm. "One hundred Thornton Lane," he said to Olivia. "Six thirty. Please come. Please," he added, his eyes a combination of intensity, pleading, worry and hope.

Yes, please come and talk my father out of finding the woman he's meant to be with, the very woman Olivia had been searching for six weeks so she could fulfill her promise to her mother.

Oh, heck, she thought. What was she supposed to do? She wasn't about to tell the Fords that the woman in question was her aunt. But how could she not? And she certainly did understand Carson's concern for his dad. But what if her mother was right about Edmund and Sarah?

What if, what if, what if. The story of Olivia's life.

Not that Carson was waiting for an answer. He was already heading down the street, holding the toddler in one arm, pushing the stroller with the other. The boy's own little arms were wrapped around Carson's neck. His son sure loved him. That feeling swirled inside Olivia so strongly it obliterated all other thought.

Six thirty. One hundred Thornton Lane. She knew the house. A mansion on a hill you could see from anywhere on Blue Gulch Street. At night the majestic house was lit up and occasionally you could catch the thoroughbreds galloping or grazing in their acres of pasture. Sometimes over the past few weeks, when Olivia felt at her lowest, missing her mother so much her heart clenched, she'd look up at the lights of One Hundred Thornton and feel comforted somehow, as though it was a beacon, the permanence of the grand house high on the hill soothing her.

She didn't know what she could possibly say to Edmund Ford that his tightly wound, handsome son would approve of. But at least Olivia knew what she was doing for dinner tonight.

Chapter Two

Carson stood by the open window in his father's family room, watching his dad and Danny in the backyard. Fifty-four-year-old Edmund Ford held the toddler in his arms and was pointing out two squirrels chasing each other up and down the huge oak. Carson smiled at the sight of his son laughing so hard.

"Let's pretend we're squirrels and chase each other around the yard," Edmund said, setting Danny down. "You can't catch me!" he added, running ahead at a toddler's pace, which couldn't be easy for the six-two man.

"Catch!" Danny yelled, giggling.

Edmund let his back leg linger for a moment until Danny latched on. "You got me! You're the fastest squirrel in his yard."

"Me!" Danny shouted, racing around with his hands up.

Edmund scooped him up and put him on his shoulders, and they headed over to the oak again. Danny pointed at the squirrels sitting on a branch and nibbling acorns. Carson could hear his dad telling Danny that the squirrels were a grandpa and grandson, just like them.

Who was this man and what had he done with Carson's father? Carson's earliest memories involved watching his father leave the house, his father's empty chair and place setting at the dinner table, his father not making it to birthday parties or graduations or special events. He'd been a workaholic banker and nothing had been more important than "the office." Not Carson, not his mother, not even his mother's terminal diagnosis of cancer five years ago, leaving them just four months with her. But then came the moment she'd drawn her last breath, and Edmund Ford had been shaken.

I didn't tell her I loved her this morning, his father had said that day they'd lost her, his face contorted with grief and regret. *I always thought there was later, another day. I didn't tell her I loved her today.*

Tears had stung Carson's eyes and he gripped his father in a hug. *She knew anyway, Dad*, he'd said. *She always knew.*

Which was true. Every time Edmund Ford disappointed them, his mother would say, *Your father loves us very much. We're his world. Never doubt that, no matter what.*

Carson had grown up doubting that. But since his mother died, his father had changed into someone Carson barely recognized. Edmund Ford had started calling to check in a few times a week. He'd drop by Carson's office for an impromptu lunch. He'd get tickets to the Rangers or the rodeo. But instead of Carson's old longing for his dad to be present in his life, Carson had felt…uncomfortable. He barely knew his father, and this new guy was someone Carson didn't know at all. Suddenly it was Carson putting up the wall, putting up the boundaries.

Then Danny was born, and Edmund had become grandfather of the year. The man insisted on weekly family dinners with Carson and Danny, making a fuss over every baby tooth that sprouted up, new words, a quarter inch of height marked on the wall. And yes, Carson was glad his son had a loving grandfather in his life. But Carson couldn't seem to reconcile it with the man he'd known his entire life.

The first week of Danny's life, when his now ex-wife, Jodie, had still been around, they'd both been shocked when Edmund Ford had come to the hospital's neonatal intensive care unit every single day, to sit beside his bassinet and read Dr. Seuss to him, sing an old ranch tune, demand information from the doctors in his imperious tone.

"Grandparenting is different from being a parent," Jodie would say with a shrug when Carson expressed his shock over his dad's suddenly interest in family.

She must have been right because by the end of Danny's first week, she was gone, with apologies and "you knew I was like this when you married me," and his father was there. And everything that seemed normal about the world had shifted.

His father's housekeeper and cook, Leanna, came into the room and smiled at Carson, then walked over to the screen door to the yard. "Danny, want to help me make dessert?"

"Ooh!" Danny said. His grandfather set him down and he came running in.

The sixtysomething woman, with her signature braided bun, scooped up Danny and gave him a kiss on the cheek. Carson loved how much sweet attention his son got at his grandfather's house. "Twenty minutes 'til dinner," Leanna called out before heading through the French doors with Danny.

Carson glanced out the floor-to-ceiling windows on the opposite side of the room. If he craned his neck he could just make out the circular driveway in front of the mansion. No car, other than his own. He wondered if Olivia Mack would show up or not. Probably not.

"I could cancel my health club membership with all the exercise I get from playing with Danny," Edmund said as he came inside. He took a long sip from his water bottle, then sat down in a club chair and pulled a small notebook from the inside pocket of his jacket. "Oh, Carson, I won't be around tomorrow afternoon. I'll be on the road, checking out four potential hair salons for my Sarah."

Enough was enough. "Dad—"

Edmund held up a palm. "Well, it's what I have to do since my own son, a private investigator, won't do his job and help me find the person I'm looking for."

Carson crossed his arms over his chest. And sighed. "The person you're looking for doesn't exist, Dad."

Edmund shook his head. "We've been over this. I'm done arguing with you. I'm just telling you I won't be around tomorrow in case Danny wanted to see the more fun Ford man in his life."

His father *was* the fun one. Unbelievable. He shook his head, staring at his dad as though the concentration would help him come up with a way to reach the man, get to him to see how foolish and fruitless this quest was. And how potentially damaging. Edmund Ford was a handsome man, tall and fit, with thick salt-and-pepper hair adding to his distinguished appearance. And he was very, very wealthy. This Sarah, if he found someone who fit the bill, would latch on to him fast enough to get her hands on his bank account, then take off. She'd probably get herself pregnant, too, to keep the gravy train going for quite some time. Yes, Carson was that cynical.

The doorbell rang and Carson perked up. He glanced at the grandfather clock across the room. Not quite six thirty. Could it be the fortune-teller's daughter? Had she come?

Lars, Leanna's husband of thirty-two years and his father's butler for the past five years, appeared in the doorway. "A Ms. Olivia Mack is here." A short, portly man in his sixties, Lars always stood very straight in his formal uniform.

"Olivia Mack?" Edmund repeated. "Do I know an Olivia Mack? Is she selling something? I wouldn't mind a couple boxes of those mint Girl Scout cookies."

"I invited her," Carson said. "Show her in, will you, Lars?"

Edmund stood and wiggled his eyebrows at Carson. "*You* invited her? Finally dating? You definitely need a woman in your life."

"Not dating," Carson said. "I'm busy with raising my son and working."

Edmund rolled his eyes. "Your son is asleep fourteen hours a day. And you don't work twenty-four hours. You have time for romance, Carson."

Carson wasn't having this discussion. Luckily, the French doors opened and Lars presented Olivia Mack.

Carson had only had a head-and-shoulders view of Olivia inside the food truck. He'd had no idea she was so tall and curvy. She wore a weird felt skirt with appliqués of flowers, a light blue sweater and yellow-brown cowboy boots. Her hair, which had been up in the food truck, now tumbled loosely down her shoulders in light brown waves. A ring, bearing a turquoise heart on her thumb, seemed to be her only jewelry. Did people wear rings on their thumbs? Fortune-tellers probably did.

Olivia glanced back as Lars shut the doors behind her. She turned to Carson and offered an uncomfortable smile.

"Dad," Carson said, dragging his gaze off Olivia. "This is Olivia Mack, Miranda Mack's daughter."

Edmund Ford stepped toward Olivia. "Miranda Mack, Miranda Mack," he repeated. "Is she a loyal customer at Texas Trust? I'm sorry but the name isn't ringing a bell."

"Her mother was *Madam* Miranda," Carson said. He couldn't help but notice Olivia's eyes cloud over. She was obviously still grieving over the loss of her mother. Six weeks was nothing. It had taken Carson a good year before he got used to the fact that his mother was gone, that he would never see her again.

"Oh, of course!" Edmund said, hurrying over to Olivia and wrapping her in a hug. "I'm so sorry about your loss, dear. Your mother changed a lot of lives for the better. I understand that I was her very last client before..." He cleared his throat. "She told me the second great love of my life is out there waiting for me to find her. I intend to do just that."

"Actually, that's exactly why Olivia is here," Carson said. "To tell you you're wasting your time and energy."

Edmund frowned and turned to Olivia. "Is that right? Is that why you're here?"

Olivia bit her lip and looked from Edmund to Carson and back to Edmund. "Mr. Ford—"

"Please call me Edmund."

"Edmund," she began, "my mother's gift worked in mysterious ways. That's all I know," she added, glancing at Carson.

He grimaced at his son. "Carson begged you to come and tell me I'm wasting my time and energy on a wild-goose chase? Offered you a pile of money to make me see reason?"

"Well, he did, but I didn't accept," Olivia said. "He did also express how worried he is that you might be chasing after a fantasy that doesn't exist. I can understand that. I suppose that's why I'm here. To tell both of you that I don't understand how my mother's abilities worked. I do know that she brought together hundreds of couples. I also know there were times her predictions did not work out."

"Well," Edmund said, "I believed in her."

Carson caught Olivia's expression soften at that.

"Carson mentioned that you've been looking for the woman she told you about," Olivia prompted.

"No luck so far," Edmund said. "I've called around to a bunch of hair salons in the area, but most folks who answered the phone thought I was some nut and hung up on me. I visited several over the past two weeks, asking for a 'Sarah who I heard was a great hairstylist,' but most of the time, no Sarahs. The four times there was a Sarah, she didn't have green eyes." He let out a breath. "I guess this does sound kind of silly."

"Romantic, though," Olivia said on practically a whisper.

Carson frowned at her.

"I think so, too, young lady," Edmund said, the gray cloud gone from his expression. "And I may be fifty-four, but that doesn't mean I'm not a whiz with technology." He pulled out his smartphone. "I've got a map of every hair salon in the county with digital pushpins of ones I've visited." He held it up. "If there's no green-eyed Sarah, I've marked it red. I've got nineteen salons to visit tomorrow in two counties."

Carson rolled his eyes and shook his head. "What about the fund-raiser you're supposed to speak at tomorrow? What about the board meeting to prepare for?"

"Carson, I'm your father. Not the other way around."

"Dad, I—"

"Dinner is served," Leanna sang from the doorway with Danny in her arms. "Danny helped make dessert."

"Ert!" Danny called out.

"Dessert monster!" Edmund said, rushing over and tickling him and carrying him over his shoulder. Danny squealed with laughter.

This ridiculous quest to find this nonexistent green-eyed hairstylist was just another example of how much his father had changed, especially since Danny was born. For Danny's sake, Carson liked the devoted, fun grandpa his formerly workaholic, bank-before-family father had become. But this silly search to find a gold digger masquerading as a predicted great love? No. Not on Carson's watch.

He had about forty-five minutes to shift this conversation back his way. And Olivia Mack was his only hope of stopping his father from ruining his life.

In the biggest dining room that Olivia had ever been in, she sat across the huge cherrywood table from Carson. At the head sat Edmund Ford with little Danny in a high chair beside him. Watching grandfather and grandson did a lot to ease the tension that had settled in Olivia's shoulders ever since she'd arrived. Edmund clearly adored the toddler, and baby talk—*Who ate all his chi-chi? My widdle cuddlebomb did, that's who! C'mre for your cuddlebomb!*—was not beneath the revered banker. Olivia hadn't known what to expect from Edmund Ford, but this warm, welcoming man was not it.

The three generations of Fords looked quite alike with their dark thick hair, though Edmund's was shot through with a distinguished silver. The three shared the same intense hazel-green eyes.

"Edmund, how did you happen to become a client of my mother's?" Olivia asked. She smiled up at Leanna, who walked around with a serving platter of roasted potatoes. As the woman put a helping on Olivia's plate, she wondered what it would be like to live like this every day. Maids and butlers and a family room the size of the entire first floor of Olivia's house.

"When I moved to Blue Gulch four years ago, a year after my wife passed," Edmund said, "I would hear this and that about a Madam Miranda and didn't give it a thought. To me, fortune-tellers were about crystal balls and telling people, for a fee, what they wanted to hear."

"And you were right," Carson said, fork midway to his mouth.

Edmund ignored that. "But then I overheard a few conversations that stayed with me," he continued, taking a sip of his white wine. "A very intelligent young equity analyst at the bank was telling another employee that she went to see Madam Miranda about her previous job and whether she should dare quit without having another lined up first. Madam Miranda advised her to quit immediately because an old college friend who worked at Texas Trust would call about an opening there and she would apply, interview and be offered the job with a significant increase in pay. Oh, and she'd love working there. The analyst risked quite a bit by taking that advice. Three days later, an old college friend called. And the rest is history."

Carson was doing that thing again where he rolled his eyes *and* shook his head. The double dismissive whammy.

"I would catch some stories like that," Edmund said, "and I just sort of tucked them away, not having any interest in paying Madam Miranda a visit."

"What changed your mind?" Olivia asked, taking a bite of the rosemary chicken. Mmm, that was good. So well seasoned. Olivia hadn't had a meal she hadn't cooked herself in a very long time.

"About two months ago, I overheard two young women talking in the coffee shop," Edmund said. "I was waiting for my triple espresso, and I heard a woman say that Madam Miranda's prediction for her had come true, that if she'd find the courage to break up with her no-good, no-account boyfriend, she'd find real love with a handsome architect whose first name started with the letter *A*."

"Oh, come on," Carson said, shaking his head.

Edmund kept his attention on Olivia. "The young woman went on to say she'd been dating the terrible boyfriend for two years but Madam Miranda's prediction gave her something to hope for, even if it was silly and couldn't possibly come true, despite being so specific. She dumped the guy, and three months later, she struck up a flirtation with a young man doing some work in the new wing of the hospital where she worked as a nurse. An architect named Andrew."

Carson put down his wineglass. "Madam Miranda probably heard his firm would be working on the new hospital wing. She put the idea in the nurse's head that she and this guy belonged together and voilà, instant interest when she might have otherwise ignored him."

"Talk about far-fetched," Edmund said to his son.

"I have a million of those stories," Olivia said. "I've seen much of it firsthand. And my mother may have been a lot of things, but a liar or a cheat wasn't among them."

Carson put down his fork. "Right. So my father's second great love is a stranger named Sarah standing in a hair salon giving some guy a buzz cut. Come on."

"Why not?" Olivia asked. "Why isn't that possible?"

Carson sighed. "Because it's hocus-pocus. It's nonsense. It's make-believe. It gets people to pony up a pile of money for malarkey—and just like that nurse said, it gives hope where there's none. It doesn't mean a damned thing."

"Watch your language," Edmund said, covering Danny's ears. The boy giggled.

"Larkey!" Danny shouted gleefully.

"How much did you pay the madam for this fantasy?" Carson asked his father. "Hundreds, no doubt, once she knew who you were."

"I've told you at least three times that she refused to accept money from me," Edmund said, taking a bite of his chicken. "She told me she thought my bittersweet story was deeply touching and that was payment enough."

Olivia knew her mother often didn't charge those who clearly couldn't afford her services. But Edmund Ford was a zillionaire. His story really *must* have touched Miranda—or had her mother known that he was destined to become part of the family because of Aunt Sarah? Hmm.

"But," Edmund continued, "considering that her fortune-telling parlor was inside her home, which was on the small side, a postage stamp, really, I left her a thousand dollars in cash anonymously. She deserved it."

The head shaking was back. "Right, Dad. I'm sure that's how she hooked, lined and sunk her wealthy clients, pretending to care, finding their pasts just so touching, and fully knowing they'd load up her mailbox with cash and gifts. Payment enough—ha."

"Could you *be* more cynical?" Edmund said, once again covering little Danny's ears and making the boy giggle.

"I'm not cynical, Dad. I'm realistic."

"Who's ready for desserty-werty?" Edmund said to Danny, kissing his soft little cheek. "I know I am!"

"Me!" Danny shouted.

Olivia glanced at Carson, who was brooding in his

seat. She'd say for this round, each man had scored a point each. They both made sense.

Carson let out a breath and shook his head, crossing his arms over his chest.

Edmund stood and lifted Danny out of his high chair and set him down. "Sweets, why don't you go play with your toys for a few minutes until Mrs. Hilliard brings out dessert."

The boy went running for his toy chest, surrounded by brightly colored bean bags and low bookshelves.

"Right after I overheard that young lady telling her friend about finding true love," Edmund said, "I started having all these strange feelings." He glanced at Carson. "About wanting that for myself. I loved your mother, Carson. Very much. The last eighteen months especially, I've found myself changing, becoming very family-oriented when I wasn't before."

Carson glanced out the window, but Olivia could tell he was listening.

"After five years as a widow," Carson continued, "with a new appreciation for loved ones, I found myself longing to find love again. And so I made an appointment with Madam Miranda to see what she might say about my chances."

Carson let out a deep breath. "It's not that I don't want you to find love again, Dad. I just don't want you to go on some crazy wild-goose chase and end up getting hurt by a gold digger."

"I know you care, Carson," Edmund said, his tone reverent. "And I appreciate that you do. But I believed Madam Miranda. I consider myself a pretty good judge of character and that woman looked me in the eye with truth."

It was like a hug. After Carson's criticism of her mother, after her own years and years of trying to find some rational explanation for her mother's abilities, to hear her last client say this with conviction in his voice was like the warm hug that Olivia had needed for six weeks. Her only other family member—Aunt Sarah, very likely Edmund Ford's second great love—was somewhere out there, long out of hugging distance.

"Will you stay for dessert?" Edmund asked her.

She took another glance at Carson. The man was scowling. His plan to have her derail his father's belief in her mother's fortune hadn't exactly worked.

"I'd better get going. Thank you for dinner," she said. "I'm so glad we got to meet."

"Well, rest assured that I will make good on your mother's prediction for me," Edmund said. "I will find my green-eyed, hair-cutting Sarah." Olivia smiled and he took both her hands in his. "I'm very sorry for your loss, Olivia. I know how it feels to lose someone you love so deeply."

What a dear man he was. "Thank you."

"I'll see you out," Carson said between gritted teeth.

"Bye, Danny," Olivia said, smiling at the toddler.

"Bye!" Danny said with a smile and a wave and his grandfather joined him in his toy area.

As she and Carson walked through the marble foyer and out the front door, Olivia could tell Carson was waiting until they were outside to let her have it for not backing him up. She could feel the tension in him.

But all he said, while looking around the circular drive, was "Where is your car?"

"I walked, actually. My car is almost fifteen years old and might not have made it up the hill to the drive."

He seemed surprised. "I'll walk you home. Let me just tell my dad and Danny I'll be gone for a while."

"Oh, you don't have to—"

"I insist," he said.

Now he'd have a half hour to give her an earful about how she'd messed up the one thing he wanted.

"I suppose you feel like I got to eat that amazing rosemary chicken and roasted potatoes and perfectly timed asparagus for nothing," Olivia said as they headed down the hill toward town.

Carson raised an eyebrow and glanced at her, struck again by how lovely she was. She had a delicate, fine-boned face and her long light brown hair framed it in waves. The cool breeze blew her sweater against her full breasts and he found himself sucking in a breath at how sexy she was. Flower-appliqué felt skirt and yellow cowboy boots and all. He realized he was staring at her and glanced ahead at the twinkling lights in the distance, where the shops and restaurants of Blue Gulch Street were just winding down. How could he be attracted to her?

"Meaning, I don't think your dad will give up on the quest to find this woman," Olivia said.

"Well, I appreciated that you came and were fair," Carson said. "It's not like you were necessarily on either our sides." He felt her looking at him. "And I don't think he'll give up, either. I've tried for two weeks now, ever since he first mentioned it to me. You were my last hope."

"Two weeks? My mom's been gone for six, and I know their appointment was just days before she passed away."

"He said he tucked the fortune away, let himself really think about it, and then decided he was ready to see if it was possible, if there really could be a second great love out there."

"Carson?" she said, darting a glance at him. "Is the reason you're so against his trying to find the woman because of your mother?"

"My mother died five years ago. I don't begrudge my father love or companionship. It's the fortune-telling aspect that I have problems with."

"My mom tried to keep a list of all the marriages she was responsible for. Her last count was three hundred twelve."

Please. "I don't believe that."

"You don't believe much," she said.

That wasn't true. He believed in a lot. In his love for his son. In doing his job and helping bring criminals to justice by tracking them down for the police. In the way Olivia Mack's big brown eyes drew him, making him unable to look away from her face.

Olivia looked past him toward the beautiful horse pasture. The thoroughbreds weren't out tonight. "Did you grow up in that house?" she asked.

"No, I grew up in Oak Creek." A town over, Oak Creek was the fancy cousin of Blue Gulch, filled with estate ranches and mansions. "My father sold the family house a year after my mother died. He said the memories were killing him and he needed a fresh start and had always liked Blue Gulch with its quaint mile-long downtown."

"Ah," she said. "That's why I haven't seen you around. I think just about everyone in town has been to the food truck in the two weeks it's been open."

"I meant to tell you—the shrimp po'boy was pretty darn good. I have no doubt that word of mouth will bring in business from the surrounding towns."

She smiled. "Thanks. My mother's business worked that way, too. Word of mouth brought in client after client, just as it did with your dad. Relative and friends came in from neighboring states, too, for a chance to meet with Madam Miranda."

"So tell me how this supposedly works. Your mother had this magic ability to predict the future but it wasn't passed down to you?"

"According to my mother, all the women on her side of the family have a gift," she practically mumbled.

"What number am I thinking of?" he asked.

She smiled. "I have no idea."

"So what is your gift?" he asked.

"That's a lovely tree," she said, eyeing the weeping willow at the edge of the Ford property. She clearly didn't want to talk about this.

He leaned toward her. "You can read minds. You can move objects with your eyes. You can make yourself invisible."

She laughed. "None of the above. I'm not sure I want to talk to about it, Carson. I've struggled with believing it myself, but based on what I've seen with my own eyes, I seem to be able to affect people with my cooking."

What? "Your cooking?"

She nodded. "Aside from running the Hurley's Homestyle Kitchen food truck during the week, I'm a personal chef. I seem to be able to change moods and lift hearts with my food."

She glanced at him, and he tried to make his expression more neutral but the disappointment punching him in the stomach made that impossible.

"Not what you want to hear, I know," she said. "But this is my family. This is me. I'm not saying I understand it or even want it, but I seem to have this…gift."

He resumed walking, shoving his hands in the pockets of his leather jacket. "You made me a shrimp po'boy. What effect did that have on me?"

"I don't think any. Which is unusual."

He *was* disappointed. For a moment there, despite everything, he'd felt drawn to this woman. But here she was, spouting the same nonsense her mother had. He wanted to walk away, but he wasn't going to just abandon her in the evening on the sidewalk, even in very safe Blue Gulch. He'd been raised to be a gentleman.

So he'd play along. Maybe he'd trip her up, get her to admit how ridiculous the idea was. Lifting hearts with her food? Lord. "So how do you set this up? You offer customers a chance to turn their frown upside down for an extra five bucks?"

She shot him a glare. "Did I say one word to you when you ordered? No. I don't charge extra. I just get a sense of what someone needs and I infuse the food naturally. Maybe an insecure person will get a boost of confidence. A hurting person will feel a bit stronger."

"And a pissed-off man like me, worried about my father wasting his time and energy on some crazy fortune? Why didn't the po'boy change my mood?"

She bit her lip and looked down at the ground. "I really don't know."

"Shocker."

"You don't have to be rude," she said, crossing her arms over her chest.

Right then, under the darkening sky, the combination of her hurt expression and how alone she seemed made him feel like a heel. "Sorry. I'm just…my father is new to me, Olivia. My whole life, until my mother died, my father was a stranger I barely saw. Work was the most important thing in his life. Now, he's a different person. Kinder, interested in family, in people, in the community and world around him. I once thought he had no heart, and now he has too much heart. You see how he is with Danny."

She tilted her head. "Can a person have too much heart? He's wonderful with Danny. A dream grandpa."

"All that extra heart means a lot more room to be hurt and easily swindled." He stopped walking for a moment, struck by what he'd just said. He hadn't realized how worried he was that his father would be hurt—not just swindled. The man who made Danny laugh and shout "yay!" whenever Carson mentioned they were going to see grandpa was not going to get that heart stepped on by a con artist.

"I think my mother meant every word of that fortune, Carson."

Why was she so frustrating? Who cared if Madam Miranda believed in her phony "gift"? There was no such thing as predicting the future. There was probability and possibility and plain old-fashioned guesses. But there was no crystal ball. "Right, Olivia. So somewhere out there is a green-eyed woman named Sarah in a hair salon with some ridiculous blow-dryer tattoo. And she's my supposedly my father's second great love."

Olivia nodded. She seemed about to say something, then looked away.

"Well, I'm not going to let my father go on some

wild-goose chase and let some swindler snow my dad for his money. I finally have my dad. I'm not going to let him get hurt."

"Or you could have a little faith, Carson Ford."

He rolled his eyes. "I'd laugh but I don't want to be rude again."

She lifted her chin. "I live just down this street," she said, pointing to Golden Way. "Please thank your father for his hospitality." Then she stalked off.

He watched her walk to the second house on the left, a tiny yellow cottage with a white picket fence and a bunch of wind chimes. A black-and-white cat was sitting on the porch and wrapped around her legs, the yellow-brown cowboy boots. Olivia bent down and scratched the cat behind the ears, then picked it up and gave it a nuzzle before carrying it inside.

When the door closed, he felt strangely bereft, the lack of her so startling that he wanted to knock on the door and argue with her a little more just to be near her.

He had to clamp down on that feeling. He'd been through the wringer with his ex-wife and had no interest in feeling anything for a woman. Everything he had, all the mush and gush he had left, went to his son. Olivia Mack was likely in on her mother's scam, though she did strike him as honest, and Carson considered himself a pretty good judge of character, of sizing someone up.

She wasn't going to help dissuade his father from heartbreak and a big time-waster. Which meant he had to forget Olivia Mack and the way she got under his skin.

Chapter Three

By twelve thirty in the afternoon the next day, Olivia had sold thirty-seven po'boys and thirty-two cannoli. Not bad for an hour's work. Being so busy in the food truck had taken her mind off a certain tall, sexy PI. She'd barely slept last night, tossing and turning as she thought about all Carson had said, all his father had said, her mother's prediction, her aunt Sarah, who she missed terribly. Carson was a complicated man. The situation was complicated. But cooking wasn't complicated at all. You followed a recipe and there you had it. Simple.

She stood at the cannoli station, which was a two-foot-long section of stainless-steel counter, and added a dusting of powdered sugar to a mini strawberry cannoli.

"Here you go," she said to Clementine Hurley Grainger,

who sat at the swivel stool at the tiny desk near the cab of the truck.

Twenty-five-year-old Clementine's dark eyes lit up and she put down the stack of receipts she'd been going through. "Ooh, that looks amazing—thank you." She took a bite. "Absolutely delicious!"

Among Olivia's favorite words.

Clementine took another bite, then put down the cannoli. "I'm amazed by these receipts!" she said, picking up a few. "One order alone was for seven cannoli—and not even the lower-priced minis!"

Olivia smiled at her friend and one-quarter boss. Clementine's grandmother, Essie Hurley, owned Hurley's Homestyle Kitchen, where Clementine was a waitress. Clementine had had the brilliant idea for the food truck while on a family honeymoon with her new husband, Logan Grainger, his twin three-year-olds and the foster daughter they were in the process of trying to adopt. On a road trip across Texas, everywhere they stopped there were brightly colored, inviting food trucks with long lines of customers. One family meeting later, some numbers crunched with Georgia Hurley—Clementine's sister, who baked for the restaurant and handled the books—and creating the menu with Annabel Hurley—their other sister and the lead chef for the restaurant—and the food truck came into existence. Working with the three Hurley sisters and Essie to get the truck ready for business had given Olivia such purpose the past weeks.

"Mandy from the real estate office bought those," Olivia said as she sautéed onions, celery and garlic for the next batch of pulled-pork po'boys. "She says they tend to put clients in signing mode." And for the past week, one o'clock meant she'd have a line of hungry customers from Texas Trust, the employees at the coffee shop, plus the construction crew working on a house just around the corner that always ordered three po'boys per guy.

"We get compliments on your po'boys and cannoli all the time at the restaurant," Clementine said. "I can't tell you how many times I've heard people say, 'I could be in the worst mood, have one of Olivia's cannoli and suddenly have a skip in my step.' Whatever you're doing, keep doing it. Gram is thrilled with the success you've made of the truck."

"I'm so happy to hear that," Olivia said. "I don't know what I would have done without this new venture to focus on and throw myself into. I owe you and your sisters and grandmother everything."

"We're even, then," Clementine said, taking another bite of her cannoli. "Ooh, hot construction workers coming your way," she said, upping her chin at the group of six men walking toward the truck. Olivia laughed. "Well, I'd better get to work myself. See you later."

By two o'clock, Olivia had made over a hundred po'boys and seventy-five cannoli, which was up since she'd started offering the mini cannoli.

"Excuse me, but I was here first!" a grumpy female voice snapped.

"Actually I was, but please, go ahead," responded a familiar deep voice.

Olivia peered out the window, setting aside the head of lettuce she was about to rip apart. A thirtysomething woman was elbowing Carson out of her way, jockeying for position in front of him at the food-truck window. Carson moved behind the sourpuss, who was busily texting so fast, with such fury on her face, that Olivia was surprised the phone didn't explode from the sparks.

"May I help you?" Olivia asked the woman. She glanced past the woman at Carson. He wore cop-like sunglasses and his leather jacket.

No response.

Olivia cleared her throat. "Next!" she called out, which always woke people up.

"Meatball-parm po'boy with extra parm," the woman grunted without looking up from her phone. "And two mini cannoli, one chocolate with chocolate chips on the ends and one peanut butter."

There was anxiety under the woman's anger, Olivia knew suddenly. Someone close to her—a boss? A teenager?—was driving her insane.

"Do you want me to take the test for him?" the woman screeched at the phone, shaking her head. She seemed to be yelling at a text she'd received. "Never get married," she said to Olivia, fury on her face. "Then you'll never have to deal with an idiot ex-husband who blames you for your fifteen-year-old's F in chemistry and D in Algebra Two."

Olivia tried for a commiserating smile. "Your order is coming right up," she said, heating the meatballs in the sauté pan. She scooped them out onto the baguette and layered the sauce—her aunt Sarah's old recipe—and then added the Parmesan cheese, then another layer, per the request. She could feel a shift in the air around the po'boy and knew her abilities were at work. Exactly how the woman would be affected was a mystery.

Olivia handed over the order in a serving wedge and the woman stalked over to the pub table a few feet away.

"She practically ran me over since her face was glued to her phone," Carson said, stepping up to the window. "She even stepped on my feet with those clod-hopper cowboy boots."

Olivia smiled. "How are your toes?" She bit her lip. Was she flirting? She didn't want to flirt with Carson Ford.

He smiled back. "They'll survive."

"Oh, God," the grumpy woman said from her table. She held up the po'boy and examined it, taking another bite, letting the Parmesan cheese stretch high in the air before gobbling it up. "Oh, my God, this is good." She inhaled the rest of her po'boy, then sipped her water and took a very deep breath, exhaling as though she was meditating. She held up one of the cannoli. "This almost looks too pretty to eat, doesn't it?" she said cheerfully to Carson.

"It looks very edible, actually," he said.

The woman laughed as though that was hilarious. She took a giant bite of the chocolate cannoli. Then a bite of the peanut-butter one. "Scrumptious. Absolutely scrumptious!" She grabbed her phone and pressed in numbers. "Donald Peachley, please. I don't care that he's in a meeting. Tell him it's an emergency." Olivia eyed Carson. "Donald, your ex-wife here. I have an idea. Let's get DJ a tutor and we'll split the cost. Since I make twenty percent more than you, I'm even willing to pay twenty percent more…Great…Bye now." She then popped the rest of the chocolate cannoli in her mouth, quickly followed by the peanut-butter one.

Olivia smiled at Carson. An innocent smile. An I-told-you smile.

"Excuse me," Carson said to the woman. "But I'm curious about something. You seemed very upset five minutes ago. But you came up with a good solution to your problem and handled it very well," he said in a fishing tone.

"Well, I know what a cheapskate tab-keeper my ex is, so I figured if I offered to pay a little more for the tutor he'd go for it. It's funny, though—before lunch I never would have been so...reasonable or generous. I've been accused of being my own worst enemy. Can you believe that?"

Carson didn't answer that. "So you probably had low blood sugar, had some food and felt better, which got you thinking clearly."

"Low blood sugar? I had two slices of pizza at Pizzateria ten minutes before I came over here. When I'm furious, I eat."

Carson scowled.

"Something about these cannoli always peps me up," she said. She glanced at her phone. "Back to the grind. See y'all."

Carson crossed his arms over his chest. "People like cannoli," he said to Olivia. "It's a pick-me-up. That's all there is to it."

"I agree," Olivia said. "That's how I look at it most of the time. Until I start thinking about how my food seems to have such specific effect on people. Then I start to doubt myself as a doubter."

And the more Carson insisted her gift was malarkey, the more she was forced to acknowledge that it wasn't. Deep down she'd always known and didn't want to acknowledge it. But she did have some kind of gift to restore through food.

Except maybe when it came to this man.

"What can I get you?" she asked. "Special today is pulled pork. I have six kinds of sauces. And the cannoli of the day is the peanut-butter cream."

"I actually came to tell you that I made a decision about my father and the prediction. My dad has business he can't just blow off this week. Which is crazy because when I was growing up, I would have loved for him to put his personal life before work. Now here I am, insisting he honor his commitments. I'm going to track down his Sarah for him."

Olivia froze. "You are? I thought the last thing you wanted was for him to find this mystery woman."

"I'm going to find her for him because I can do it quickly—it's my job to find people. And when I do find her and he feels absolutely nothing for her, I can prove once and for all that the fortune is a bunch of hooey. We can both get on with our lives."

Well, that sounded cynical, but everything inside her lit up at the idea of reuniting with her aunt. "So you've started the search?" she asked.

"No. I'll do some research tonight and hit the road tomorrow. I need to make this quick. I have a pending case and people counting on me."

"I'll help," she said. "And come with you to find her."

"What? Why would you want to do that?"

Olivia took a deep breath. She had to tell him. "Because this green-eyed hairstylist named Sarah with the brush-and-blow-dryer tattoo sounds exactly like my estranged aunt."

The hazel-green eyes narrowed.

* * *

Disappointment conked him over the head, then fury punched him in the stomach so hard he almost staggered backward.

He stared at Olivia and then turned and stalked away.

"Carson, wait!" she called.

He kept walking, wanting to put as much distance between himself and the lying, swindling Mack women as possible. A daughter, a mother, an aunt. All in cahoots.

"Carson!" she called and he could hear her chasing after him. "Please hear me out!"

He noticed some people stopping on the sidewalks, pausing in their window shopping. Busybodies.

He kept walking. He would not hear her out. There was nothing to hear. Of course she'd said she'd help him find "Sarah." He had no doubt Olivia Mack knew exactly where her aunt was. This was all probably one great big ruse to make this air of mystery around Sarah's whereabouts so that his father was pulled in even more. No one wanted what came easily. Damn, they were good at being lying swindlers. They reeled in Edmund Ford and now were playing the game, putting the aunt out of his reach just until the fantasy would take over any issues with reality. At this point, his father was in love with the fantasy. She was his predicted second great love, and that's all he'd need to know.

"Carson, please!" she called.

He kept walking, the cool February air refreshing against the hot anger spiraling inside him. He'd parked his car on a side street, and when he reached it, he got in and sped off toward Oak Creek.

When he opened the front door of his house, he

could smell apple pie in the air. Danny's sitter had made two pies with her little helper, and he was now napping. He let the sitter know he would be doing some research, then tiptoed into Danny's room. He watched his son's chest rise and fall, his own tense shoulders relaxing. Watching his son sleep never failed to relax him.

In his office, he sat down on the brown leather couch and pulled out his cell phone to call his dad and tell him this Sarah person was just Olivia's aunt and the fortune-teller's sister. And what a nice parting gift to hook up the family with a wealthy widower.

Cheap shot, Ford, he chastised himself.

He punched in his dad's cell number.

"Edmund Ford speaking."

"Dad, I just found out this supposed second great love of yours is the fortune-teller's sister. Clearly, you've been set up."

"Her sister?" Edmund said.

"Olivia told me the person Madam Miranda described sounds a lot like her estranged aunt. Down to the name, the job, the eye color and the tattoo."

Silence. His father was a smart man. Clearly he now knew this was a ruse and he probably felt exactly like Carson had on the street—sucker punched upside the head and in the gut.

"That's great!" Edmund said. "That means we have a last name! Maybe even a Social Security number to help track her down. And a physical description beyond eye color. This is great news."

Was Carson the crazy one? "Dad, are you telling me you don't think the fortune-teller made up this crazy prediction to land her sister a wealthy widower?"

"I did this to you, didn't I?" Edmund said.

"Did what?"

"Made you so cynical."

"Do you mean realistic?" Carson asked. "And yes, you probably did. But being realistic is a good thing, Dad. Being grounded in reality is a good thing."

"I'm going to find my Sarah with or without your help."

Click.

Without or without your help.

He'd heard those same words from Tug Haverhill, his neighbor at their old house in Oak Creek. Tug had two sons around the same age as Carson but he'd always invited Carson to throw a football or to come fishing. When Tug's younger son had turned eighteen, he'd run off to—according to a note he'd left—"see the world my way." Apparently, Tug Haverhill had been around a little too much for Brandon Haverhill, insisting Brandon follow the path he'd laid out—a certain college, then business school while working in the family corporation, and he had a great gal in mind for him, too, the daughter of a board member. All that had worked on his older son, but not Brandon.

When Carson had become a private investigator working for the Oak Creek police department, Tug had offered him a small fortune to find his son and bring him home "just to talk." Tug had told everyone in town that he'd hired Carson to find Brandon, and when Carson and Brandon arrived on the Haverhill doorstep a few days later, word spread that Carson could get the job done. Unfortunately, Brandon had come only to tell his father he'd never live his life any way but his own. His father was furious and Brandon left again. Carson had felt for Tug Haverill, who never did let go of his need to be right. In the end, folks only remembered that Carson had found Brandon when no one else could. He'd been hired to find everyone from long-lost relatives to runaway dogs to deadbeat dads to people like Brandon, who simply walked away from their lives without looking back.

Carson had never got the message. You held on too loosely, you lost people. You held on too tightly, you lost people. There was a "just right," Carson supposed, but he'd never mastered it. He'd tried both with his ex-wife, then found himself awkwardly saying and doing things that hadn't felt anywhere near right, and none of that had worked, either. His wife had left.

She left her own newborn, too, his father had reminded him. *That's not about you. That's about her.*

Well, Carson has chosen her, hadn't he? He'd fallen in love with a woman who had it in her to walk out on her own baby—and supposedly because the baby was a boy and not the girl she wanted. A boy who looked like Carson instead of her and was so frail he needed to be in the NICU for six weeks. In those acid-burning weeks that followed, Carson had pledged to put his son before all else; if he ever fell in love again, it would be with Mary Poppins.

But Mary Poppins was fictional, so Carson had pretty much spent the last year and a half alone.

Also fictional? The nonsense Olivia Mack was spouting about her shrimp po'boys and chocolate cannoli having magical powers. The entire Mack family were clearly nut-jobs and there was no way in hell he was leading to his father to one of them.

Carson stood. Yes. He'd find Sarah Mack himself to keep his father from missing important events this week. He'd assess her and introduce her to his father, who'd feel absolutely nothing for the fortune-teller's gold-digging sister, and voilà.

He entered the name *Sarah Mack* into Google, then realized he didn't even know if Olivia's aunt was married or not. A simple search brought him many Sarah Macks, but they were all either too young or too old to be Olivia's aunt. He tried "Sarah Mack, hairstylist" and there were two, but both were under thirty.

It would be a lot easier to find the woman if he knew more about her. That was one of the keys of finding people, he'd learned—you needed to know the little details. Something Carson had discovered early on was that people liked to be reminded of home even when home meant strife or bad memories or they thought they were running as far from home as possible. Once Carson had a sense of what meant home for someone, figuratively speaking, it made it much easier to find them.

And to learn something about this Sarah Mack, he needed some information from Olivia.

He stood up, grabbed his jacket, let the sitter know he'd back by six, then headed for Blue Gulch and Olivia Mack's little yellow house.

Chapter Four

Olivia sat on the red velvet divan in the back room of her house—her mother's fortune-telling parlor. After Carson had stalked off, she'd tried to reach him a few times, but he wouldn't answer his phone. She'd been so disconcerted by telling him the truth about the mystery woman and by his expected reaction that she'd gone home after her shift and thought she'd soak in a bubble bath and try to think about how to go from here. But instead she'd been drawn to her mother's parlor.

Olivia had always loved and hated this room. Loved it because it was very much her mother. The rich velvets and satins, the small treasures from her travels around the country and the world. Miranda Mack actually did have a crystal ball. She'd found it in a secondhand shop owned by a tiny woman who'd celebrated her hundredth birthday the day Miranda celebrated her seventeenth and had come into the San Antonio store. According to Miranda she'd picked up the ball and it had glowed, and the shop owner had smiled and said Miranda should take it as a birthday gift from one birthday girl to another. It now sat in its bronze holder on the rectangular table in the "fortune nook," separated from the main room by heavy red velvet drapes. The nook was like a mini version of the main room, full of red velvet and treasures dotting the walls and sidebars. As a girl, Olivia had always felt very safe and protected in the nook.

But then she'd turned seventeen and knew that was when her own gift, passed down from the maternal side of the family, would make itself known, and Olivia had been freaked out. She wanted to be like Aunt Sarah, who claimed not to have a gift and insisted the family abilities must skip around. But Olivia's ability to heal with food had presented itself, at first, imperceptibly. Sarah always refused to talk about the family gifts and Miranda would shrug, but Olivia always thought there were family secrets being kept from her. If only she *could* read minds.

Sweetie, her mother's old cat and her cat now, jumped up on the sofa and curled up beside Olivia. She gave the cat a scratch behind the ears and reached for one of the many photo albums her mother kept on the coffee table. She stared at the last bunch of photos of Aunt Sarah, a tall, pretty woman with wildly curly auburn hair, her signature scarf tied around her neck. In one photo she wore a skin-tight black dress, the little tattoo visible on her ankle. In another photo, Sarah had her arm around Olivia and was smiling at her with such love in her warm green eyes.

What could have happened between the Mack sisters to make Sarah run off? To estrange herself from her only sibling and the niece she'd seemed to care so much about?

There was a knock on the door—the back door, where her mother would meet her clients. Surprised, Olivia jumped up. She moved aside the layers of gauzy curtain at the door to see Dory Drummond wearing a T-shirt, jeans and a long white wedding veil. Dory, recently engaged after a whirlwind courtship, was an old friend and often helped Olivia with cooking prep for her clients or in the food truck to make some extra money.

Dory's expression was a combination of worry and resignation, but there was a smidgen of something else…but what?

She wants to do what's right but she isn't sure what that is.

Whoa. The thought slammed into Olivia so forcefully she took a step back.

Olivia opened the door. "Dory, what's wrong?"

"I'm sorry to bother you at home. I stopped by the food truck to ask if we could get together to talk sometime soon, but a guy said you were off." Olivia noticed she held the telltale yellow paper bag from the Hurley's truck. "I have two smothered, chicken-fried-steak po'boys if you're interested."

Olivia smiled. "One of my favorite kinds, especially when I didn't have to make it." She gestured at the round table by the window and Dory sat down, Olivia across from her.

Dory stared at the yellow bag. "I've been dieting since I've been engaged. But you know what? A Hurley's Homestyle Kitchen smothered chicken-fried-steak po'boy sounds amazing, which is why I couldn't resist ordering it. My mother used to make chicken-fried steak and mashed potatoes in her incredible gravy every Sunday night." Tears poked at Dory's eyes and Olivia had to blink back her own. The losses of their mothers was something they'd gone through together. But over the past few days, since Dory had gotten engaged, Olivia had the feeling Dory was avoiding her.

"I miss my mother's cooking, too," Olivia said, reaching over and giving Dory's hand a squeeze. Granted, Olivia was the cook in the family, but when Olivia was a little girl, her mother would make her food into smiley faces on her plate, cut holes in pancakes for strawberry eyes and a sausage mouth. And every night for as long as Olivia could remember, her mother would make them both a cup of lemon-ginger tea and they'd watch TV together or sit on the little porch with the cat in Miranda's lap. Olivia missed that so much, but she still wasn't ready to have lemon-ginger tea.

Dory squeezed her eyes shut, then opened them. "Okay, I'm just going to tell you. I have to tell you. I don't know what to do."

"Of course you can talk to me," Olivia said.

"Your mother is the reason I'm here."

Oh, no. Not again. Carson Ford was enough to deal with where Miranda Mack had been concerned.

Olivia sighed inwardly. She noticed Sweetie pad over and stare up at Dory. "Sweetie is, like, eighteen years old, but I'm afraid she might leap on the table and swipe at your beautiful long veil."

Dory's mouth dropped open and she reached up and felt the veil, her expression telling Olivia she'd forgotten it was on. She looked around, clearly embarrassed, took off the veil and folded it neatly into her tote bag.

"It was my mother's," Dory explained. "I tried it on at home…to see what it looked like, to know what it would feel like, and I got so… I guess I ran out to go to talk to you without realizing it was on. I must have looked like the biggest idiot running through town in a wedding veil."

Got so…didn't sound so good, Olivia thought.

"I'm sorry to just barge in on you like this," Dory said, her blue eyes full of worry.

"That's okay, Dory. Really."

Dory opened up the bag and slid out the po'boy and took a bite. "I'm not supposed to be eating this. Beaufort's mother made an appointment for me with her nutritionist and personal trainer. I'm only supposed to eat whole foods so I look my best for the wedding." She took another big bite. More tears poked her eyes.

"Dory, what's going on?" Olivia asked. Beaufort was her fiancé. From one of the wealthiest families in town, Beaufort had his eye on running for mayor and then state senate.

Dory reached down to pet Sweetie as though to prolong saying why she was here. "I never told you this, Olivia, but I went to see your mother just two days before she died. I asked her to tell me what she saw for me, and she looked me right in the eye and said she adored me like a daughter, but she couldn't hold back the truth to spare feelings or hopes and that I wasn't in love with Beaufort Harrington."

"Oh, no," Olivia said, her gaze drawn to the three-carat diamond ring sparkling on Dory's finger. "Did she say more?" When Madam Miranda made her pronouncements, she usually didn't elaborate. *People know the truth about themselves deep down*, her mother had always said. *I tell the truth. Some people either can't handle the truth or don't want the truth and they do as suits. Others can't deny what's just below the surface.*

"When Beaufort proposed, I was so surprised," Dory continued. "I thought for sure he'd throw me over for a woman more like his family—rich and cultured and all that. I mean, it was always kind of obvious to me that Beaufort had a crush on me but he'd never asked me out until just two months ago. Then he proposed a few days ago and I said yes…for a few reasons."

Huh. "Is love one of them?"

Dory hung her head. "My mother didn't have health insurance. Her care took everything. I've been working 'round the clock to pay off those bills and keep the bakery going. Can you imagine, Olivia, losing my mother and my father—and then the family business? Drummond's Bake Shop has been in my family for seventy-five years. I can't lose it. I told Beaufort all this, that I was in a heap of trouble financially and that he wouldn't want to marry someone in such financial straits, and he said he'd make all my financial problems go away."

"Because he loves you so much?" Olivia asked.

"I'm not sure if he does or not. I always ask why an ambitious, handsome banker from a wealthy family would pick me, of all the women in Blue Gulch, and he just says I'm what he wants." She shrugged. "I don't know. We don't have all that much in common. I can't quite figure out why he *did* propose."

"Well, maybe the reason *is* love," Olivia said.

Dory nibbled the po'boy. "I don't think so," she

whispered. "I know this is going to make me sound terrible, but it kind of made me feel okay about saying yes. He doesn't love me but wants to marry me for some reason. I don't love him, but need to marry him for a reason. I suppose we're both doing the other a favor. But…your mom telling me what I already knew—what she must have known I already knew—is throwing me. She must have focused on that for a reason."

Olivia stared at Dory, this lovely, petite blonde with angelic blue eyes and a sweet manner. She wanted Dory to have everything—her family bakery, love, her financial worries gone. "Did my mother say anything else?"

Dory shook her head. "She only said that I wasn't in love. She said it again as I was leaving." Tears filled her eyes. "I'm all alone in the world, Livvy. And just like in a fairy tale, a knight in shining armor rides up."

Except Dory didn't love her knight in shining armor. *Sometimes people don't want the truth and they do as suits…*

Dory's use of her childhood nickname made her heart clench. As teenagers, they used to spend so much time talking about the kind of man they wanted to marry someday. Being madly in love with someone who was madly in love back was first on the list.

"I'm sorry I dumped this on you," Dory said, putting her half-finished po'boy back in the bag. She stood up, slinging her tote bag on her shoulder. "I just needed to say it out loud to someone who I knew wouldn't judge me or advise me. I just needed to get it out, you know?"

Olivia stood up and went around the table and hugged her friend. "I know. And I know you'll do what feels right to you, Dory. Whatever that may be."

As Dory hugged her back, the doorbell rang. "I'll let you go, Liv. Thanks for listening."

Dory left and Olivia went to the front door. Carson Ford stood there. She was relieved to see him. And barely able to take her eyes off him. How could she be so drawn to a man who was so…her opposite?

"Isn't that Dory Drummond?" Carson said, upping his chin at Dory, who was getting into her beat-up old car, which was even older than Olivia's.

"Yes, she's an old friend. Why?" Olivia asked.

"She just got engaged to a close family friend," Carson said. "Beaufort Harrington. Our fathers go way back."

Just figures, Olivia thought. She would definitely keep quiet about the fact that Dory had been a client of her mother's.

"Carson, look, I really am sorry about all this with my mother and my aunt and your father. But I promise you, there is nothing underhanded about it. My mother wasn't that kind of person."

"Then help me prove it," he said. "I intend to find this Sarah person myself so that my father's life isn't interrupted or upended. I'll find her, introduce them, my dad will feel absolutely nothing for this stranger and he can go back to his life and I can go back to mine."

"How can I help?" she asked. "I've been trying to find my aunt Sarah since my mother died."

"We can start with her last name, Social Security number if you know it, details that will narrow the field."

"I've tried all that. Well, not her Social Security number. I don't know it."

"Well, then we're going to take a road trip."

* * *

Carson stood on Olivia's porch, unsure if he'd really just said those words. A road trip with Olivia, who he barely knew?

"Do you have a day off coming up?" he asked. "We can make some calls, find out which salons employ Sarahs and go check them out."

She opened the door wider. "Come on in. Coffee?"

"Biggest mug you have," he said, stepping inside.

He glanced beyond the small foyer to see a tiny living room with a green velvet sofa, a well-worn oriental rug and all kinds of decorations, from masks to little statues. Madam Miranda clearly hadn't been raking in the bucks, given the old scuffed wide-plank floors and the unrenovated kitchen he could see through a doorway. Interesting.

"Did you grow up here?" he asked, following her into the small kitchen. She gestured at the round white wood table by the window and he sat down.

"I was born in this house. I've lived here all my life."

"Did you used to listen in when your mother was telling fortunes?" he asked.

"I tried not to," she said. "To give her clients privacy. But sometimes I couldn't resist." She poured chocolately-smelling coffee grounds into the coffee-maker and pressed a button. "One time, my middle school science teacher came to see Madam Miranda. Mrs. Flusky was the meanest teacher at the school, never smiled, barked at kids. I eavesdropped when she came. It took her a good five minutes to ask her question. She said, 'How can I go on with this pain of losing my daughter?' I don't think anyone knew that Mrs. Flusky even had a daughter. But it turned out her daughter was just twenty-two when she was hit by a car."

He saw Olivia wince just saying those words. "What did your mother tell her?"

"My mother told Mrs. Flusky that by going on, by living her life, by teaching with passion, by going back to the activities she'd given up, like her book club and her garden and traveling, she would be honoring her daughter by honoring *life*. Which would always have its share of crushing sorrow, its days of the status quo and, of course, joy. Madam Miranda then asked Mrs. Flusky how she thought her daughter would feel to know that she'd given up all she used to enjoy because of her grief. Mrs. Flusky said her daughter would hate knowing how small and sad her life had become, that they'd been planning to travel the South together that summer, but of course she wasn't going."

Carson leaned forward, curious what else Madam Miranda had said.

"And then my mother reached under the table and pulled out a small flowerpot," Olivia continued. "She told my mother to plant her daughter's favorite flower in the pot. When the flower bloomed, that meant it was time for Mrs. Flusky to honor her daughter by blooming anew, respecting the new person she was in the face of the changes in her life, but by doing what she enjoyed. She also gave Mrs. Flusky three flower seeds and said she'd bet her daughter would love it if she planted each seed in the three places they'd planned to visit in July."

"And did Mrs. Flusky change? Did she go on the trip?"

"I waited every day to see a difference in her. Finally, after a few weeks, she came into the classroom with the flowerpot my mother had given her. There was a green shoot. She put it on her windowsill in the sun. And she was different from that day. Not in any big way, but she was nicer. She even smiled sometimes. And I'll never forget how she said that when the school year ended she was going to Atlanta, Savannah and Charleston." She set out two mugs of coffee, along with cream and sugar.

He added cream and a spoonful of sugar. "You do realize there was no fortune-telling involved there," he said. "No hocus-pocus. Just compassion and insight."

She nodded. "I do realize that. I thought about that session for a long time. Before that and after that I'd heard my mother tell people their fortunes, what she saw for them. But with Mrs. Flusky, she told her what she *needed*. When I understood that, I knew for sure that my mother was the real deal, Carson. She wasn't a con artist. She cared. And I also began to realize that she did tell people what they needed—whether through a fortune or just common sense. If what she saw wasn't what they needed, she wouldn't put it out there."

"So my father *needs* your aunt Sarah." He leaned his head back.

"He must," she said. "Crazy as that sounds."

"As long as you know it does sound crazy," he said, surprised to find himself giving her something of a smile.

He could see her visibly relax, her shoulders drop a bit. He felt like a heel for making her so tense, for storming into her life and making his family's problem hers, especially when she must still be grieving her mother's loss. He wanted to get up and go over to her and press his hands on those shoulders and massage away her tension.

She wore a white T-shirt with a faded ad for Blue Gulch Animal Rescue, the silhouettes of a dog and cat on her stomach. Her skirt was some kind of denim-patch thing and she was barefoot, a silver ring around one of her toes. He followed her tanned legs from the toe ring up the toned calves to where the skirt ended. He'd been physically attracted to women before, of course, but something about Olivia Mack drew him in a way he hadn't experienced in a long, long time.

He cleared his throat for no reason other than to shake himself out of his sudden fantasy of walking over to her and kissing her. He pulled out the little leather notebook with its tiny pen that he carried everywhere. "Is your aunt Sarah's last name also Mack?"

She nodded. "She wasn't married when she left town. Her name was Sarah Mack, no middle name. But I've done many online searches for her, putting in all kinds of search words, like hair salons, her name, et cetera. Nothing ever comes up."

"You referred to your aunt as your estranged aunt," he said, sipping his coffee. "What's the story there?"

Olivia sipped her own coffee. "I don't know the whole story. There's a big family secret I've been kept in the dark about. But I do know that my aunt told my mother she was never, ever to tell Sarah her fortune—she didn't want to know, she wanted to do what felt right to her, make her own mistakes. Maybe there came a time when my mother couldn't hold her tongue?" She shrugged. "It's complicated, that's all I know."

Her aunt sounded levelheaded, so that was a plus. He

wouldn't want to know his supposed fortune or future, either. "Do you think she's still in Texas?"

"I don't know for sure, but I suspect. Sarah loved Texas. She was a big rodeo fan."

"Oh, yeah?" he said. "That's a good start. People tend to run away to what comforts them. Tuckerville is a bustling town full of shops and restaurants and it borders Stockton, where the rodeo championships are held. Seems a good place to start." Tuckerville was just an hour away. Two hours driving, two hours visiting salons. Half a day's work and hopefully they'd find her.

"So we're going to just get in your car and go visit hair salons in Tuckerville and ask for Sarahs?"

He nodded.

"I'm off tomorrow," she said. "But I need to cook tomorrow afternoon for Mr. Crenshaw. It's his chicken parmigiana and garlic bread night. He counts on it."

Carson had no idea who Mr. Crenshaw was. "I'll have you back home by three. How's that?"

"Mr. Crenshaw likes to eat at five thirty. Getting home at three will be cutting it very close."

"I'll help you," he said. "I'm a pretty good cook. I've had to learn these past eighteen months for Danny's sake."

She tilted her head and stared at him for a moment. "Okay, then. Most hair salons open at ten, so why don't we leave at nine tomorrow morning."

Half a day's work and this nutty situation would be resolved. He figured, anyway. But he was well aware that for someone who wanted this lunacy finished and done with, he sure was looking forward to spending time with Olivia tomorrow.

Chapter Five

Olivia sat on her porch at nine sharp, waiting for Carson. A shiny black SUV pulled into the driveway and he hopped out to open the passenger door for her. Gallant, she thought, offering him a smile as she got inside.

"I bought us coffee," he said as he buckled up and pointed at the two foam cups in the console cup holder. "One cream, one sugar, right?"

For a moment she felt flattered that he'd noticed and had tucked away how she liked her coffee, then she remembered it was his job to notice details.

"Thanks," she said, taking a sip and glancing at him as he started the engine.

The bright sun lit his dark hair and she saw shades of brown and copper. He slid on aviator sunglasses that made him look like a state trooper.

"So where's Danny this morning?" she asked as they headed toward Blue Gulch Street.

"He goes to a day care he loves three mornings a week. He has two best buddies there. My dad will pick him up today and keep him until I return."

"Your dad is so great with Danny. So loving. I never had grandparents. My mother's mother died before I was born and no one ever talked about my grandfather. I didn't know my father or his family."

He looked over at her. "I didn't know my grandparents, either. It's one of the reasons I'm so protective of my dad right now. For Danny's sake."

"I can understand that," she said. "Your son is lucky to have you."

He glanced at her again and was quiet for a moment, then said, "When Danny's mother walked out on us, I was so worried that I wouldn't be enough as a dad. I mean, I know I'm not a laugh a minute. Not that my ex was, either, but she was very outgoing and bubbly. Thank God my dad morphed into an award-wining grandfather."

His ex-wife walked out on them? Olivia couldn't imagine. Hadn't Carson said his son had been in the NICU for a couple of months? Had his mother left while Danny had been in the hospital? She wanted to know more about Carson and his past, but she wasn't sure she should pry.

There was suddenly a hard set to his jaw and shoulders so she figured she'd better keep the conversation to their mission. She already thought too much about Carson, wondered too much, noticed him too much. "Did you let your father know that you're looking for Sarah?"

A muscle worked in Carson's jaw and he shifted. "I did."

"And?" she prompted, sipping her coffee.

"He was a little too touched," Carson said. "Even though I made it clear I'm not doing this to find his supposed second great love. I'm doing it to prove that he'll feel absolutely nothing for this woman so he can go back to living his life."

"What if he *does* feel something?" Olivia asked. "Yes, I know, power of suggestion, blah, blah, blah. But you can't fake chemistry, a pull toward someone, a quickening of your pulse, an inexplicable draw."

She knew because she felt it with Carson. She couldn't stop stealing peeks at him, the strong profile, the broad shoulders, the muscular thighs.

"It would be pretty random for my father to meet some stranger and fall instantly in love. I have no doubt he'll feel toward Sarah Mack the way he feels when he meets anyone. The earth won't move."

"What if it does?" she asked.

He looked at her, clearly frustrated. "It won't."

She couldn't help a chuckle. "You sure are set in your ways."

"You are, too."

"Nope," she said. "I'm open to possibility."

He didn't respond to that. He reached into the inside pocket of his leather jacket and pulled out a piece of paper. "This is a list of every hair salon in Tuckerville and the surrounding towns. There are six in Tuckerville. And then four more in the bordering communities. I called ahead—there are four stylists named Sarah in four of the salons. Two in the bordering towns. My dad didn't come out this far in his search. We very well may find your aunt this morning."

She glanced at the list, her heart skipping a beat.

Was Sarah Mack in one of these salons? Tears poked at her eyes, and Olivia realized she wanted to be reunited with Sarah so badly that it was overwhelming.

"We're here," he finally said, turning onto a bustling main road and pulling into a spot in front of a bakery. When she didn't move, he glanced at her. "Hey," he whispered. "Are those tears?" He lifted up her chin and brushed away the wetness under her eyes with the back of knuckle. "We'll find her."

For a moment she was so startled by his kindness that she just stared at his hand, now resting on his knee. "We want to find her for very different reasons," she said. "You want to end something. I want something to begin."

He nodded, then gave her hand a squeeze. "Well, that may be true. But at least you'll have her back, right?"

Olivia froze. "What if she doesn't want to be found? I mean, she clearly doesn't."

Carson turned off the ignition and turned to face her. "You know what I've learned most in my business of finding people? That ninety-nine percent of people who walk away *do* want to be found, even if they don't know it, even if they're not walking around with it burning in their chest the way it can be for the people doing the looking. It's not easy living with something unsettled—on either side."

"Ninety-nine percent," she repeated, liking that number.

He nodded and was around the car to open her door for her before she could even hitch up her purse on her shoulder.

Feeling a bit better about what might happen, she

got out and looked around. The busy downtown was divided by a four-lane road, with shops and restaurants dotting both sides. Tuckerville was a lot bigger than Blue Gulch.

"Hair Magic is two shops down," he said, pointing left.

Hair Magic. Nope. No way. Aunt Sarah, who hated magic, hated talk of the family gift, would not work in a salon with the word *magic* in the name. That she was a hundred percent sure of. She was about to tell Carson they should cross it off the list, but there it was, Hair Magic, right between a heavenly smelling bagel shop and a bookstore.

And anyway, what did she know about her aunt, really? Maybe she did work here. Maybe the word *magic* was just another word. Aunt Sarah had never been superstitious or sentimental. And it had been five years since she'd seen her. Five years. She used to think she and her aunt were close, but Sarah had walked away from her. Olivia and Sarah had never had an argument; it wasn't fair, but wasn't that the old line about life?

Hair Magic had a storefront painted silver with silver drapes in the window. A bell jangled as they entered. There was a reception desk with no one behind it and six hair stations; two women and one man, all in various stages of their work, had customers. A Shania Twain song was playing from a speaker on a sideboard with magazines laid out across it.

"Are either of the women your aunt?" Carson whispered. "They look young."

She shook her head. Both women were in their twenties. Aunt Sarah was forty-eight.

"Can I help you?" one of the women called out.

"I heard there was a hairstylist who works here named Sarah who's great with men's hair," Carson said.

Olivia supposed that was his line to get info.

The man beamed, which told Olivia he was the owner and liked the word-of-mouth praise for one of his employees. He eyed Carson's hair, which was thick but relatively short. "Sarah doesn't come in until ten thirty. If you want to wait, I'm sure she can squeeze you in before her eleven o'clock client."

"Could you describe her?" Carson asked. "My friend said Sarah is in her forties. Auburn hair?"

"That's Sarah," the man said.

Olivia's heart squeezed. Aunt Sarah worked here. She was coming in a half hour!

"Bingo," Carson said. "That was easy," he added on a whisper to Olivia. "We'll wait," he said to the owner.

Could it really be this simple? Olivia liked simple, but when was anything this easy? Their first day out, their first hair salon, their first try? Aunt Sarah materializes through a Tuckerville doorway?

They sat down on the padded bench. Olivia watched the man pull a big round brush through a blonde's wavy hair, straightening the tresses. She glanced at the clock on the wall—10:02 a.m. The anticipation was too much. This would be a long thirty minutes.

Carson took a little notebook from his jacket pocket and flipped through it. He nodded a couple times, jotted something down, then returned it to his pocket.

"What's your aunt like?" he asked.

Olivia thought of tall, strong Aunt Sarah. "Well, she's a bit private and always kept to herself, but when I was growing up she'd come see me a few times a week, help me study, take me shoe shopping, bring me MP3 players loaded with songs she thought I'd like. When I was getting my catering business off the ground she would post flyers for me in shops and bulletin boards all over Blue Gulch County. She sent me quite a few of my first customers."

Carson glanced at her. "She sounds kind."

"She is." Olivia wanted to add, *See, you don't have to worry about your dad and Sarah, she's wonderful, really.* But Carson would just say there would be no "Dad and Aunt Sarah" and cross his arms over his chest and glower, so she kept that to herself.

They sat and watched a woman get her highlights wrapped in foil and listened to the chitchat. Olivia now knew all about an affair going on in the stylist's family, the client's teenaged son's struggles in language arts class and how many bottles of color number twelve the salon needed to order.

"Have any earplugs?" Carson leaned over to whisper.

Olivia couldn't help but smile. She actually liked all the chatter and gossip and chitchat. She always worked alone—for years in her kitchen, cooking for her clients, and for the last few weeks in the food truck. *It's lonely,* a little voice acknowledged. Before, she'd go home to her mother, who never stopped talking. Now she went home to a silent house and constant reminders of her losses. *I do want to find you, Aunt Sarah*, she thought suddenly. *Very much.*

The bell jangled, and Olivia almost jumped. She glanced up at the big clock on the wall—10:25 a.m. Aunt Sarah? She looked over at the woman who entered. She was tall, like Sarah Mack. Auburn-haired, like Sarah Mack, though her aunt's hair was curly and this woman's was pin-straight. Of course, a flatiron could have made that happen. Big black sunglasses covered her face.

Olivia hadn't seen her aunt in five years, but she felt sure that she'd know her aunt anywhere. And this woman…wasn't Sarah Mack.

Olivia stayed in her seat, disappointment prickling her heart.

"Sarah Mack?" Carson said, standing up.

The woman turned to Carson and took off her sunglasses. Dark brown eyes looked at him quizzically. "Sorry. I'm Sarah O'Dalley."

Carson's shoulders slumped. "Oh. Sorry to bother you. I was looking for a different Sarah." He asked if the stylists knew of any Sarahs who worked out of their homes, but no one was sure.

Olivia finally stood up and he glanced at her, his expression softening at the sadness she couldn't hide from her eyes, the dashed hope. He put a hand on each of her shoulders. The heavy warmth felt good.

"Sorry," he said as they headed for the door. "I should have asked the owner if her last name was Mack before we bothered waiting." They stepped out into the bright sunshine. "But then again, she may have married and changed it—or changed it even if she didn't marry. We'll find her, though."

"I don't know," she said. "If a person doesn't want to be found…"

"It's one salon," he said. "Three more to check with Sarahs, and we can go to the other two just in case she changed her name entirely. If she's not in this town, we'll just keep looking. We'll find her."

Olivia shrugged. She wasn't so sure.

He stared at her for a moment. "You really miss her, don't you?"

She nodded. "She's my only family. My mother didn't marry my father and he just sort of disappeared before I was even born. I mentioned I didn't have grandparents. For the longest time it was just me, my mom and Aunt Sarah." A chill snaked its way around her body.

"And now it's just you," he said.

She nodded, looking away. "I had no way of getting in touch with Sarah about my mother's death. And I tried very hard to find my aunt then. Maybe it's wrong to look for her. Maybe I should respect her wishes."

"Except now it's about your mother's wishes," he said gently.

Yes. That was exactly it. She felt so comforted by the fact that he understood that she almost threw herself around him.

Until she remembered he had his own reason for finding Sarah Mack. And it had nothing to do with the last promise she made to her mother on her deathbed.

"We'll find her," Carson repeated with conviction. "I promise."

That was a big promise. And she'd do well to remember he was motivated by self-interest—saving his father from possible heartbreak and financial ruin by finding his supposed second great love so that his father could see there was nothing between them. That Sarah was just a stranger.

An hour later, Olivia and Carson had visited the five other salons in Tuckerville. There were three Sarahs. None was Olivia's aunt. They stopped in a coffee shop to ask around if anyone knew of a freelance stylist named Sarah who worked out of her home, but no one did.

"For all we know, my aunt is working in a salon across the state, nowhere near a rodeo," Olivia said as they walked out of the coffee shop. "But it was a good try. She did love watching the rodeo."

Carson stared at her for a moment, gently pulling her out of the way of a man walking six dogs. "You know what we need?" he asked.

"What?" Olivia asked.

"Lunch."

She smiled. She was pretty hungry now that she thought about it.

He glanced around at the many restaurants and cafés on both sides of the main street. "Fancy or the bagel place for chicken salad on everything bagels?"

"The bagel place," Olivia said. "For tuna salad on a sesame bagel."

He nodded and took her hand, leading the way. His hand tight against hers felt so good she wanted to kiss him.

Grr. She had to be careful where Carson Ford was concerned. It was one thing to appreciate a man's handsome face and rock-hard body and deep voice and so on and so on, with Carson's many physical attributes. It was another to have her heart responding to him.

And it was, darn it.

As Carson turned on Blue Gulch Street, he remembered that he'd promised Olivia he'd help her cook for whoever this Mr. Crenshaw was.

"So what did you say we're making Mr. Crenshaw?" he asked as he pulled behind Olivia's car in her driveway.

"I won't hold you to helping me," she said. "If you need to get back to your work or go pick up Danny, I'll understand."

"I spent three hours early this morning on the case I'm working on. And my father complains he doesn't get enough time with Danny, so it's fine to leave them together for a couple extra hours."

"Well, then, we're making chicken parmigiana with garlic bread and a side of linguine in red sauce, one of Mr. Crenshaw's favorites. I make it from a recipe his wife had handed down from her great-grandmother."

As they headed inside Olivia's little house, she explained about her clients and their various dietary plans. Mr. Crenshaw was her secret favorite, she said. An eighty-seven-year-old widower who lived at the local assisted-living center but grumbled about the food. So Olivia cooked for him three times a week at a very big discount.

The moment Carson stepped through the doorway, the black-and-white cat weaved between his legs and he reached down to pet her. She rubbed her head against his shin, her long white whiskers stark against his charcoal pants.

Olivia smiled. "If my mother had witnessed that, she'd say you were okay, that Sweetie knows her people."

Carson raised an eyebrow. "A psychic cat. Just what the world needs."

She laughed, the sound making him happy. She hadn't laughed much today.

He followed Olivia into the kitchen, aware of the sway of her hips in her skirt, the way the late afternoon sun streaming in through the bay window lit the brown hair that hung in waves past her shoulders. She handed him an apron but he was so busy staring at her lips that he dropped it.

He scooped it up. "Olivia Mack, Personal Chef and Caterer" was embroidered in white script along the big red pocket.

"Put me to work," he said. "Should I be on linguine or chicken?"

"If you could take care of the linguine and the salad, I can focus on the chicken. My kitchen is yours, so just open the fridge and cabinets at will."

He wasn't really that much of a cook. He made breakfast and dinner for him and Danny every night. French toast was Danny's favorite so that was in heavy rotation in the mornings. As were homemade chicken fingers with sweet potato French fries for dinner. Then there was his mother's meat loaf recipe. Spaghetti in marinara sauce. Omelets stuffed with cheese and vegetables, which Danny gobbled up. He could handle linguine and a salad, though he doubted it would be up to a personal chef's usual level.

An array of pots and pans dangled from a rack above the stove. As he moved to the cabinets to search for the pasta pot, he brushed against Olivia, who was pulling the chicken breasts from the refrigerator. He wanted to take the chicken out of her hand, toss the pot and lean her up against the fridge and kiss her senseless. He wanted to but, of course, he pretended great interest in filling up the big pot with water. He glanced over at Olivia, and she glanced at him.

Had she felt the jolt, too? Had she felt nothing? He had no idea. Usually he could tell when a woman was as attracted to him as he was to her, but Olivia seemed very neutral to him. *Too* neutral, given what had brought them together and was still before them in finding her aunt.

He smiled. Maybe she was just as attracted.

"Thinking of something?" she asked as she covered the chicken in flour.

"I'm thinking that it's very comforting to watch someone cook. My mother was a great cook. She was obsessed with Julia Child and making her way through her giant cookbook. No chicken fingers for me as a kid. I was eating beef bourguignonne at three. Danny's probably lucky I'm not a great or adventurous cook. He hates mushrooms."

Olivia laughed. "Your mother sounds wonderful."

"She was," he said. "Did you learn to cook from your mom?"

She shook her head. "Madam Miranda wasn't much of a cook, but she had a few favorites that she learned to make. Cooking was never big in my family."

"Who taught you?" he asked as he set the back burner to high.

"I just always knew. When I was five, I could make a three-course dinner."

Her "gift," supposedly. Which Carson didn't want to think about or talk about. People had talents. Olivia's was cooking. End of story.

"Won't Mr. Crenshaw be disappointed when he tastes my rubber pasta and marinara sauce without enough pepper?" he asked as he salted the water for the linguine.

She eyed the pot. "You seem to know what you're doing. And besides, I'm watching. Closely."

He stopped stirring the linguine and stared at her. There was the slightest hint of flirtation in that last word. Her cheeks flushed and she turned back to her chicken. Suddenly she was very involved in making homemade bread crumbs and seasoning them. Hmm. Maybe she was as aware of him as he was of her.

He had the urge to walk up behind her and smell her hair. Breathe her in. Wrap his arms around her. When he used to think about what marriage would be like, he used to think about that. Doing boring everyday things, but while making out.

He turned his attention back to the water. Marriage. Ha. Marriage had gotten him all alone with a son who lately had been saying, "My mommy?" And because Carson knew exactly what Danny was asking, he wasn't going to pretend he didn't just because it was so damned painful to answer.

You have a mommy, he'd say. *But she had to go away.*

Mommy back? Danny would say, his hazel-green eyes just curious, not sad, not heavyhearted like his father's always were. Danny had never known his mother and at eighteen months, he was still young enough not to realize that something wasn't right about why his mother wasn't in his life.

All I know for sure is that if your mother knew you, she'd be unable to stay away from you, Carson would say, his heart feeling like it might implode. Explode.

Choc bunny? his son would say then, and relief would flood Carson's veins and he'd hand him the little chocolate bunny he'd bought as a treat and let Danny nibble an ear.

Danny's sweet face came to mind, his absolute trust in Carson. What was he doing, thinking about kissing Olivia Mack? Romance and love led to heartache and loss, and Carson had taken himself out of the running for that end result. He needed all the room in his heart for Danny.

Somehow he'd have to resist Olivia Mack. He'd make the salad, get the sauce going and then he'd leave. Olivia could handle the garlic bread.

Except as he was opening the fridge to find the lettuce, she was about to do the same and they collided. She was a half inch from him, flour on her cheek. Before he could think, he leaned down and kissed her, then took her face in his hands and deepened the kiss, opening his eyes when he dragged his mouth away from hers, dying to see her beautiful face.

She wrapped her arms around his neck and he kissed her again, harder, longer, and backed her against the counter, the scent of her soap and seasoned bread crumbs assailing him.

Sweetie the cat meowed so loudly that they both pulled back and stared down at the black-and-white cat staring up at them with her amber-stone eyes.

"You did say the cat was psychic," he said, stepping back. "So clearly it's a sign that we shouldn't be..."

"She's not really psychic," Olivia said and he tried to read the expression in her eyes, but all he got was *neutral*. She was good at masking how she felt. Or maybe this wasn't such a big deal. A hot kiss in a hot kitchen. That's all it was. He just didn't go around kissing women in kitchens or anywhere, for that matter. So it was a big deal. And he had the feeling it was for her, too.

"If I'm late with dinner, Mr. Crenshaw will pace the hall at the assisted-living center," she said. "So we should really get back to cooking."

He opened the fridge again and pulled out the lettuce. And a cucumber. And the tomatoes. He reached around Olivia's sexy form for a knife and began chopping and slicing. Once the salad was done, he asked Olivia about dressing, but apparently Mr. Crenshaw liked plain old olive oil and vinegar, which he had in his room. It turned out that Olivia had made the marinara sauce that morning, so he was done here.

"I guess I'll be in touch when I have some news about your aunt," he said. "Now that I have the basic information and the photos you gave me, I can work on my own."

"Oh," she said, the neutral expression back on her pretty face.

He might have thought she really didn't care either way, but the set of her shoulders, the way she held herself so stiffly, told him she did. He wanted to go over and massage them, tell her that he was just…what? Closed off? Closed, period? Refusing to start something he couldn't finish because he didn't want to hurt her? And that he would hurt her because he didn't believe in romance or love anymore? Yes. All that.

"Okay," she said, turning to face him for a moment before laying a piece of mozzarella cheese on the chicken. He could see the cloud in her eyes. "Thanks for helping."

He nodded. "See you around," he said and shot out of there. But he stood on her porch for a good long minute, wishing he could go back inside and prolong what they *had* started.

Chapter Six

Olivia had not heard from Carson in two days. She assumed that meant he hadn't found her aunt and was still looking. She also assumed that meant he regretted his impulsive kiss.

She didn't.

All day today and yesterday she'd hoped he'd come to the food-truck window, but he hadn't made an appearance. That kiss had been hovering in the air between them for a while and she thought it was better that it was acted on than ignored. *Ignoring the truth is among the worst things for your health*, her mother used to say.

So Olivia hadn't ignored the truth of her growing feelings for Carson Ford on all levels and when he kissed her, she kissed him back. Two days ago, while they'd been cooking together in her small kitchen, she'd barely been able to concentrate on Mr. Crenshaw's chicken parmigiana. In fact, she'd been so focused on her feelings for Carson that she must have infused the chicken with some passion because one of the assisted-living nurses reported that Mr. Crenshaw had asked a lady to dance at the weekly social for the first time since arriving two years earlier.

She was sure she'd see Carson tonight at the engagement toast Dory's mother-in-law-to-be had quickly put together for family and close friends in the Harrington mansion, where Olivia was now helping Dory get ready. Like Dory, though, Olivia was used to being part of the staff as a caterer in homes like this one, but tonight, the party was in Dory's honor and Olivia was a guest whose only job was to mingle and sip champagne. Since Carson had mentioned that his family and the Harringtons were old friends, she was sure he and his father would be here.

"Zip me up?" Dory asked, looking everywhere but at her reflection in the ornate gold standing mirror in the corner of Dory's "dressing room." Beaufort's mother, Annalee Harrington, had insisted Dory prepare for the party at the mansion, as it was always referred to, in her own special "readying room." Dory had called Olivia and begged her to come to the party an hour early for support more than anything.

Olivia zipped up the back of Dory's stunning midnight blue velvet dress. She stood behind Dory in front of the mirror, aware that her friend could barely look at herself. "Dory, this is all happening so fast and you seem to be getting swept up in it. If it's too fast, you can slow it down. I can let Mrs. Harrington know you're not feeling well and the party can be put off. You can have some time to really think about this."

Dory finally looked at herself in the mirror. "I have thought about it—a lot. I do like Beaufort. I'm sure I'll grow to love him. We have nothing in common, really, but soon we'll have family in common, right? And meanwhile, my family's bakery will be saved. After paying the last of my mother's hospital bills, I have two hundred and fourteen dollars left in my bank account. I had to let go of my last employee at the bakery because I couldn't pay another week. She was a single mother, Livvy." Tears glistened in Dory's eyes. "Beaufort picked me, the girl from the wrong side of the tracks with only a falling-down bakery to her name. That means something to me, even if it shouldn't. I think he does really love me. I'm sure I'll grow to love him."

Olivia looked at her friend's reflection. "Dory Drummond, you have a good head on your shoulders. I know you'll do right by yourself. If that means marrying Beaufort, so be it. If that means telling him you can't, so be it, too."

"Thanks, Livvy," Dory whispered with a nod.

There was a knock on the door.

"Come in," Dory called, lifting her chin and clearly trying to shake away her concerns.

Annalee Harrington swept into the room in her own exquisite dress, a tea length rose-gold silk. Her blond hair had been expertly put up into a chignon. How she walked on those four-inch heels, Olivia would never know.

"Dear, of course you'll wear *these* earrings," Annalee said, ignoring Olivia as she gestured at the dangling diamond-and-gold earrings on a velvet pad on the dresser. "I chose them specifically to go with the dress I picked out for you for tonight."

Dory reached her hands up to her ears. She glanced at the earrings on the dresser. "Those are gorgeous, Annalee, but my mother gave me these pearl earrings. I wear them for all special occasions."

Annalee frowned. "Dear, those are everyday pearls. And if I may be honest, they look a bit…" She leaned in close. "Are they even…real pearls?"

"I think so," Dory said. "Thank you for the dress and all this," she added, sweeping her arm out, "but I *am* wearing my mother's earrings."

Annalee stared at Dory long and hard, then her eyes lit up for a moment as if something had occurred to her. "I suppose it'll take some time." She glanced at Olivia and scooped up the fancy earrings and walked toward the door. "You're expected to make your entrance down the stairs at exactly six when you'll be announced as Beaufort's bride, Dory. Please don't be late."

"I won't be," Dory said, and Annalee left.

Dory frowned. "Did you feel the arctic blast in here or was that just me?"

Olivia still felt the chill in the room. "Well, you stood up to her about the earrings. So if you're going to marry Beaufort, at least we both know you won't be pushed around by Annalee."

Dory gazed at her reflection, reaching up to touch the pearls again. "Why do you think that the only thing your mother would tell me was that I wasn't in love with Beaufort? To make me acknowledge what I already know but don't want to think too deeply about?"

"Probably," Olivia said.

"I keep thinking about the difference between need

and want. I want real love. But I need to think about my present and future and make sensible decisions. How can I be sure I'll ever find real love anyway?"

It wasn't meant as a question. And it didn't matter what Olivia thought. People married for all sorts of reasons. Sometimes love was way at the bottom of those reasons. Olivia knew that one of her bosses, Annabel Hurley, had initially agreed to marry rancher West Montgomery in a deal. He'd save her family business, the restaurant, and she'd be the "perfect" stepmother his in-laws required so they wouldn't seek custody and try to take away his young daughter. They married and now were madly in love. But love hadn't brought them down the aisle. Maybe things would work out like that for Dory.

"What do you think Annalee meant by 'I suppose it'll take some time?'" Dory asked.

"I really don't know. Time for you to adjust to the big change in lifestyle?"

"That makes sense." She looked around the room. "Though I don't think I ever will. It's almost six. I'd better get ready for the big entrance."

"I'll see you downstairs," Olivia said. "You do look lovely, Dory."

Her friend smiled as best she could and Olivia slipped out of the room and down the beautiful, curved stairwell. On her way, she looked around for Carson and spotted him talking to his father and a small group of people, a few of whom she recognized as customers of her food truck.

Carson looked so handsome in his charcoal suit and red tie. Because she was staring at him, he looked over and headed her way.

"You look beautiful," he said.

"Thank you. You clean up well yourself." She had a flashback of herself pressed up against the counter in her kitchen, his lips on hers. If he was remembering, too, he showed no sign of it.

A bell jangled and everyone quieted. Annalee Harrington, flanked by her husband, stood on the first step of the staircase. "May I present my dear son's lovely bride-to-be, Dorothea Drummond. They are engaged to be married!"

Dory descended to much clapping. Olivia could tell by the look on her friend's face that she'd made some sort of peace with her decision, at least for tonight. She was engaged, the party was to toast that, and they would all do so.

After circulating a bit, Dory came up to Olivia and Carson. "I didn't know you two knew each other." Dory explained to Olivia that she and Carson had met at a fund-raiser Beaufort had taken Dory to.

"Olivia is helping me with a case," Carson said.

Reminding her that that was really all there was to them.

"Dory! Congratulations," Edmund Ford said as he walked over to join them. "Beaufort is an old family friend. His dad and I go way back to prep school, and, of course, we've been on the board together at Texas Trust for decades. I've known Beaufort since the day he was born. Good man you're marrying."

Dory smiled. "I recognize you from the bakery. How's that sweet grandson of yours? Bring him into the bakery tomorrow—I'm making his favorite rainbow cookies."

"Oh, I'll be sure to," Edmund said.

As Dory was swept away by others wanting to congratulate her, Edmund leaned close to Olivia and whispered, "Thank you for helping to look for my Sarah. I know she's your Sarah, too, and, according to Carson, you want to find her as badly as I do."

"She's the only family I have left," Olivia said before sipping her champagne. "I promised my mother I would deliver a note and a family heirloom. It means the world to me to make good on that."

"Your mother must have known you'd find her," Carson said. "Or she never would have made you promise."

Olivia almost dropped her glass. Yes. He was right. Of course her mother had known she would find Sarah. Miranda Mack would never have burdened Olivia with an unable-to-be-fulfilled deathbed wish.

"I suppose this means he's coming around," Edmund said, clapping Carson on the back.

Was that steam coming out of Carson's ears?

"I'm not coming around to believing in fortune-telling if that's what you're saying, Dad," Carson said. "But you're right—from what Olivia has said about her mother, Miranda wouldn't have made her daughter promise something she didn't think she could come through on. Simple deduction. Nothing to do with Miranda knowing the future."

"Well, whatever your reasons for finding my green-eyed hairstylist, I'm just grateful," Edmund said, his voice lower. "And it means a lot to me that you're on my side about something so important to me, Carson. Again, no matter the reasons why you're trying to find Sarah. Hope is a good thing."

Olivia could plainly see that Carson was conflicted. "That we can all agree on," she said.

But Carson placed his almost-full glass of champagne on a passing waiter's tray, said, "Excuse me," to his father and Olivia and walked away.

Carson was standing at the far end of the patio, staring at the lights that had been hung in the backyard, barely aware of the guests surrounding him, talking and laughing and sipping champagne. He made his appearance, he'd congratulated Beaufort and the family and now he wanted to go home to his son.

His father's crazy romantic quest, the engagement toast, the constant talk of love and marriage and happy endings all had Carson's stomach twisted. Every time he looked over at Beaufort and Dory arm in arm, he wanted to yell, *Don't do it! One of you will walk out on the other the minute something isn't perfect.*

The interesting thing was, every time he looked over at Beaufort and Dory, he could tell that something wasn't quite right *already.* They sure didn't look like or act like a couple in love. It was Carson's job to notice and pay attention, and body language spoke volumes. They didn't lean toward each other, into each other. They didn't stare into each other's eyes. Carson had known Beaufort Harrington a long time, since he was a kid. They didn't grow up in the same town, but their families spent a lot of time together, the two bankers glued to their phones while the boys explored backwoods and sneaked onto ranches to watch the huge bulls. For a long time, Beaufort had wanted to be a rancher but his father had said that no Harrington would be a two-bit cowboy and that was the end of that, despite the fact that Beaufort was now twenty-five years old. But every time Beaufort was around livestock and horses, his eyes lit up. The man's eyes didn't light up that way when he looked at Dory. And granted, Carson didn't know Dory, but this was not a woman excited about her pending nuptials, either.

Something was up about the engagement. He didn't know what, but it couldn't just be his so-called cynicism talking. The whole thing made him want to leave. Good love was bad. Bad love was bad. You couldn't win.

As he turned to head inside he saw Olivia talking to Dory and something shifted inside him. He felt it, an actual physical, tangible movement in his chest. She was beautiful in her pale yellow dress and strappy gold sandals, her long brown hair down around her shoulders, her full lips a pinky red. He'd avoided her for the past two days when all he was doing was thinking about her. But tonight was a reminder that he needed to just get this job done so it would be over. Including the time he'd need to spend around Olivia. He was starting to care about her—he did care about her—and he didn't want to. He was done with all that. It was him and Danny now, a unit, a twosome, and he'd devote his time and attention to his son, be the father he wished he'd had.

Olivia looked over at him just as his phone rang. His sitter.

Danny was throwing some kind of tantrum. He'd woken up screaming and yelling. Night terrors, the sitter thought. He let the sitter know he was on his way and would be there in minutes.

As he neared Olivia, he had every intention of just hurrying out toward the door but he found himself stopping.

Needing her.

What the hell?

"Danny is up and throwing the tantrum of all tantrums, according to his sitter," he whispered. "I have to go."

"I'll come help," she said and followed him out the door. "I'll text Dory that we needed to leave."

He didn't stop her, didn't say *I've got this*. For someone who didn't believe in much of anything these days, he sure did want her by his side right now.

Danny was indeed screaming his little head off. Olivia could hear him as she and Carson neared the front door of his house. The moment they entered, it was clear that the poor sitter seemed about to cry herself. As Carson took a screeching Danny from her, he tried bouncing the toddler on his hip and assuring the sitter it was all right, that Danny probably just had bad dreams or had an upset tummy. But Danny continued to cry his eyes out and kick.

Olivia watched Carson try everything in his arsenal to calm his son, but nothing worked. She wanted to take Danny herself and give something a try, but she was hesitant; she wasn't a mother and had zero babysitting experience. When the little boy let out a wail that almost split her eardrums, Olivia reached for Danny and, exasperated, Carson handed him over.

Olivia held Danny flat against her in his green footie pajamas, his head on her chest, and gently rubbed his back while singing a silly old camp song her mother used to sing when she was little about a meatball on top of spaghetti. Danny stopped fidgeting. He quieted down. When she was up to the second verse, Danny had stopped crying altogether. He peered at her, rubbed his eyes and seemed to be listening and fighting sleep at the same time.

"Again," Danny mumbled when she finished the song, his eyes closing and opening.

She was aware of Carson and the sitter staring at her as they stood by the door.

"Oh, thank heavens," the sitter whispered. "I'm so sorry I had to interrupt your evening. I should have been able to calm him down."

"It's no problem at all," Carson told her. "And you're wonderful with Danny. Sometimes it takes someone he barely knows."

That would be me, Olivia thought.

Carson said he'd see the sitter out to her car and would be back in a moment. By the end of the third run-through of the song, Danny was fast asleep. She held him against her, breathing in his baby shampoo, loving the sweet weight of him. She could hold him all night.

Carson came back in and smiled. "Baby whisperer."

She was about to say that the Mack women weren't known for that, but thought better of it. "Where's his room? I'll lay him down."

Carson led the way into the nursery. The room was painted a pale blue with stenciled sailboats lining the walls. Olivia gently lowered the toddler into the crib. He let out a sigh and continued sleeping.

They left the nursery, keeping the door ajar, and headed back in the living room. "I don't know how you did it," Carson said, "but I owe you. Big. Nightcap?"

"Actually, I'd love a cup of tea. Cream and sugar, if you have."

He nodded and went into the kitchen. She glanced

around, surprised by how cozy his house was. She hadn't known what to expect. It wasn't a mansion like his dad's house, but it wasn't a bungalow like hers. The home itself was a stately Colonial, white with a red door. The interior was toddler-friendly, with two big, plush sofas in durable brown leather, thick rugs, beanbags and floor pillows.

Carson returned with two mugs of steaming tea. She could smell the lemon from where she sat on the love seat.

"Thanks," she said, taking one of the textured blue mugs.

"I should be thanking you over and over. Now I know what song to sing him to calm him down."

She smiled and blew on the tea. *I want a baby*, she thought out of nowhere. *I want a baby of my own. A husband. A family.*

She did, she realized. She'd dated her last boyfriend for almost three years, and when he broke up with her out of the blue and proposed to a woman he'd met the week before—*when you know, you know*, he'd said— she'd been heartbroken. Her mother had tried to tell her, of course, but Olivia had refused to listen. Now, a year later, the ex and his wife were expecting a baby, per the announcement she'd read in the *Blue Gulch County Gazette*. At least he'd moved to his wife's hometown so she didn't have to see them all the time. Since then, she'd closed herself off to romance, cooking by herself, being hermit-like, determined not to meet anyone new and get her heart smashed again.

But she had met someone new. A handsome private investigator named Carson Ford. A divorced father of a little boy. And all those dreams had come roaring back to life. Marriage. Motherhood. Family. A unit.

To get the thoughts out of her head, thoughts that were dangerously veering toward a fantasy that the toddler she'd laid down in his crib was hers and that this handsome man sitting next to her was also hers, she blurted out the first thing that came to mind.

"So what case are you working on now? I mean, besides your father's."

He took a sip of his tea and set it down on the coffee table. "Well, the names are confidential, of course, but my client is a nine-year-old boy."

"Nine?" Surely Olivia had heard wrong.

"Nine. His father up and left three years ago. He left a note on the boy's pillow saying that he loved him but that the boy would be better off without him. He left a note on his wife's pillow, my client's mother, saying he was sorry but she always knew he wasn't cut out for this."

Olivia sighed. "'This' being adulthood?"

"Exactly," he said. "Marriage. Parenthood. Bills, responsibilities, not drinking himself drunk every night."

"The boy hired you to find his dad?" she asked.

Carson nodded. "He came to my office in Oak Creek. He put a shoe box full of one- and five-dollar bills on my desk and asked if it would be enough to hire me. I listened to his story and then told him that normally, no, his thirty-seven dollars in allowance and birthday money from his grandparents wouldn't be enough, but that sometimes, PIs took cases pro bono, meaning the client wouldn't have to pay. So I gave him back his shoe box and said he had himself a private investigator."

Dammit. The last of her flimsy hold on not falling hard for this man just...*poof*—vanished into nothing. Carson Ford was very kind.

"I let my young client know I'd need to talk to his mother, of course, and he said he was pretty sure she'd tell me not to bother looking for his dad, that the guy didn't want to be found. I went to see her and that's what she said, but if I wanted to waste my time trying to find him, fine."

"Any leads?" Olivia asked.

"He's off the grid, that's all I know right now. No arrests, no traffic stops, not using credit cards, hasn't applied for jobs with his Social Security number. If he's working, he's off the books."

She sipped her tea, the lemony heat soothing. "I suppose the boy knows you might not find him."

"Or that I will find him and it won't be what he expects. The man might not agree to come see his son even one time. Or he might be passed out drunk and unreachable. Sometimes you don't know what you'll find when you go looking."

She wondered what she'd find when they located Sarah. Would her aunt be bitter and cold? Unwilling to talk? Unwilling to accept the letter and family heirloom from her sister? Or would she be happy at the sight of her niece, whom she hadn't seen in five years?

Olivia had no idea how Sarah would react.

"It's brave of the boy to seek out his dad," Olivia said.

"It is, especially because his mother *did* prep him that he might not like what he finds." Carson leaned his head back against the couch, looking up at the ceiling. "Sometimes I think about Danny seeking out his mother someday. I don't know if she'll come back to see him on her own or if he'll look for her."

"I don't know how people just up and leave," she said, wrapping her hands around the hot mug to ward off the shiver that crept along her spine. "My aunt, your ex-wife, your young client's dad. It's sad enough that we lose people involuntarily. But to think about someone you love just walking away from you." She shook her head. "I'll never understand."

"Me, either," he said, reaching over to squeeze her hand.

He leaned his head back against the couch again and she couldn't take her eyes off the column of his neck, his strong jaw. She had the urge to reach up and run a finger across the hard line. "I used to think my father might as well have been gone," he said suddenly. "When I was a kid and teenager, nothing was as important to Edmund Ford as Texas Trust and the office. But he came home every night. Very late, but he came home. And he was never around on weekends and spent family vacations on the phone with the office. But every morning, every night, there he was."

"It's so hard to reconcile the man he is now with the father you grew up with," she said.

He picked up his mug. "I know. I want to be closer to him, but there's a brick wall there."

"That you built?"

He nodded. "I suppose it was a defense mechanism from when I was a kid, dealing with the disappointment of my father missing my birthday parties or school events or making promises to take me fishing and then canceling the morning of. That kind of thing."

"He sure is trying now," she said.

"That's true." He took a sip of tea. "I've narrowed down another couple of towns near the Stockton rodeo," he said, and she wasn't completely sure if he was changing the subject. Finding Sarah was about his dad, after all. "I called ahead and there are three Sarahs in the right age range. If you're free tomorrow afternoon, we could hit the road. I have a few leads on my young client's father in that area that I'd like to check out if you don't mind a brief detour."

"Tomorrow afternoon would be great," she said.

"Thanks again for everything you did tonight for Danny. Of course, now I'm going to call you at three in the morning when he wakes up with night terrors again or bad dreams or whatever this was."

Kiss me, she wanted to whisper.

But she didn't and he didn't kiss her. He did look at her, long and hard, and she thought he might be remembering their kiss in her kitchen.

"I'm sorry about the other day," he said. "When I kissed you. I have no business starting something I can't—"

"Can't what?" she asked.

"You're a really lovely person," he said. "I don't want to hurt you."

Ah. He either wasn't really attracted to her, didn't like her that way, or he just wasn't looking for something serious, and she struck him as the serious type. She had heard that one before.

"Maybe I'd hurt you," she countered.

"I'm impervious," he said and stood up.

Which meant he wanted her to leave. She swallowed back the little lump in her throat. She didn't want to leave.

Good Lord, she was falling in love with a man who'd just told her romance was off the table.

She didn't need Madam Miranda's crystal ball to know what was in her future if she didn't get a grip about Carson Ford.

Chapter Seven

The next day, Olivia had record sales of both po'boys and cannoli. She attributed it to both the day's specials—cheeseburger po'boys, a big hit with kids, and pumpkin-cream cannoli—and the gorgeous weather, a sunny, breezy fifty-nine degrees. The food truck had lines all morning into the afternoon, people with their faces tilted up to the sun as they waited.

Right before she was ready to turn over the truck to Dylan, the eighteen-year-old whiz-kid cook at Hurley's Homestyle Kitchen, a very handsome man with an adorable toddler on his shoulders came to the window and ordered a cheeseburger po'boy with lettuce, tomato and ketchup on one half, plain on the other.

"I'll bet the works half is for you, Danny," Olivia said to the little boy with a smile.

Danny grinned. "Burger!"

Olivia grinned back at her favorite toddler. "Someone is in a better mood today," she said to Carson.

"He woke up smiling and raring to play."

"Well, one cheeseburger po'boy, half plain, half with the works coming right up."

As she worked on their po'boy, she wondered what she would be infusing it with. Happiness. Love. Hope.

She wondered if it would have any noticeable effect on Carson. He'd been immune to the last po'boy she'd made him.

She added the lettuce, tomato and ketchup and sliced the sandwich, and then handed it through the window. She tried not to take his money, but he insisted and refused the change from his twenty.

"You look very nice today," Carson said. And since she had garlic mayo on her shirt and flour on the ends of her hair, which was up in some lopsided bun-ponytail, he must have really thought so. "See you at three at your house for the trip to Stockton," he added. "I'm going to drop off Danny at my dad's, then I'll swing by."

She smiled and watched him walk over to one of the tables on the town green. He handed Danny the plain half, and Danny took a bite. She watched Carson take a bite of his half. Then another, then another, then another. If any big or small changes were going on within the man, she had no idea. Danny, on the other hand, still had three quarters of his half left and was adorably, saying, "Burger!" to anyone who passed by. When they finished and left, Olivia immediately missed them.

Penny Jergen, the local beauty queen and barista who'd been teary-eyed over her cheating fiancé last week, sashayed over to the food truck and ordered a veggie po'boy on whole-grain bread and announced she was now doing restaurant reviews for the *Blue Gulch County Gazette* and would be giving the food truck her highest rating of five stars. *Good for you*, Olivia thought, glad that Penny had found a new outlet for herself.

Finally, Olivia passed the reins to Dylan, zipped home for a shower and found herself putting on a little mascara and a touch of lip gloss. She looked through her closet for what to wear, something nicer than jeans but not dressy, something not sexy but not unsexy, then realized that just about everything she owned wasn't sexy, but was very much "her." Like her knee-length flippy yellow skirt with the tiny bulldogs all over it. Aunt Sarah loved bulldogs, and it seemed a good omen to wear it. A tank, a light white cardigan and her red ballet flats, and she was ready.

As Olivia waited on her porch for Carson, she scanned the newspaper. On the one-page People in the News section, which some folks in town called the society section, there were some photos of Dory and Beaufort's engagement toast gathering. In one of the photos was a close-up of Dory with the caption:

Dory is wearing a dress her future mother-in-law bought for her as a welcome-to-the-family gift, but she sweetly accessorized the pricey frock with a pair of dime-store "pearl" earrings her mother gave to her for her sixteenth birthday back when they lived in the Blue Gulch trailer park.

Another photo showed the trailer Dory and her parents had lived in with the caption:

Blue Gulch mayoral hopeful Beaufort Harrington proposes to trailer-park gal, taking her from rags to riches.

Weird, Olivia thought, folding the newspaper and putting it aside on the porch. Dime-store earrings? Trailer-park gal? What was that all about?

As Carson pulled up, she took the *Gazette* with her into his SUV. "Did you see the paper? There are photos of the engagement party." With some very strange captions. "If you look very closely and squint, you can even see me in one of them."

"Actually, I did see the photos. I read the paper every morning—you never know what interesting little facts will present themselves, especially if you're looking for people. Police blotters, lottery winners, arrests that don't result in convictions—and photos of random people. Like there you are in a story about Dory and Beaufort's engagement. If someone were looking for you and had no luck, there you'd be."

She buckled her seat belt and smiled at the two cups of coffee in the holder. Carson really was thoughtful. "Huh. I hadn't really thought of all that."

"Simple, but effective. Some of the most complicated things come down to simple."

"I think that's true," she said. "Thanks for the coffee."

"I got us muffins, too," he said, pointing at the bag at his side. "Coffee-cake-lemon and cranberry-almond. Take your pick."

"Can we split them?" she asked.

"I was hoping you'd say that." The smile he shot her almost made her swoon. Happy, sexy, tender, dazzling.

She wanted to caress his handsome face and kiss him, but instead she busied herself by unartfully trying to split the muffins in two.

"I didn't know Beaufort Harrington was going to run for mayor," she said. "Dory didn't mention it."

"I think it's just talk and speculation right now. Getting his name out there, seeing if he can drum up early support. He has stiff competition."

"Dory as the mayor's wife," she said, trying to picture that. "She's not much of a spotlight seeker and is pretty shy."

"Folks like that, though," he said.

Olivia shrugged. "As long as she's happy."

Carson glanced at her. "Is she? I have to say, neither of them looked particularly happy last night. I can't really put my finger on it."

Well, Olivia knew why Dory didn't look like a blushing bride-to-be, but she wondered about Beaufort now. Maybe he did have his own reasons for proposing that had nothing to do with love, either.

"Well, maybe they just figured it was time to get hitched. If Beaufort's running for mayor, having a hometown wife is a plus."

"Romantic," she muttered, unable to help it.

"I don't know, Olivia. Maybe marrying for love isn't the be-all and end-all. Maybe marrying for purpose— whether because it's time to settle down or because someone meets the checklist—is smart. You know what you're walking into."

For Dory's sake, Olivia hoped so.

For the next hour, en route to Stockton, home of the rodeo championships, Olivia and Carson ate their muffin halves and sipped their coffee and looked out the window.

"Did you ever attend the rodeo with your aunt?" Carson asked as they pulled into a spot right in front of Wild West Hair, the first salon on Carson's list.

"A bunch of times. Right before she left town, Aunt Sarah and I went to the championships here in Stockton. She particularly loved watching the bull riders. Logan Grainger, the husband of Clementine Hurley Grainger, one of my bosses, used to be a champion bull rider."

"I didn't know that. I certainly couldn't last one second on a bull."

She tried to imagine Carson Ford on a bucking bull, but couldn't. She smiled at the thought. Carson was all man, but he was no cowboy.

A minute later, they were walking into Wild West Hair. The Sarah employed as a stylist was not their Sarah. Nor was their Sarah at Cut and Curl, or at Hair Parade. Stockton wasn't a big town and only had a small downtown that had grown out of necessity from the rodeo. Tuckerville, just five minutes away, had all the shops and restaurants. But they'd already visited the Tuckerville salons.

Dejected, they stopped in an old-fashioned coffee shop and sat at the counter and ordered coffee. Olivia smiled at the lady sitting one seat over and flipping her newspaper—and then her eye caught on a half-page advertisement.

Sarah Monk, expert hairstylist, is now at Style Mile in nearby Leeville! Over twenty-five years' experience. A master stylist of the whole kit and caboodle, including precision cuts, blow-outs, Japanese straightening, artful highlights, long-lasting color and quick cuts for fidgety children with overgrown locks. Hours: Tues–Thurs 10–6 and all day Saturday. Call for an appointment today!

Olivia's heart leaped. Sarah would use a phrase like *kit and caboodle*!

"Carson, look! Maybe Sarah's using the last name Monk. It's very close to Mack and is sort of apt. Maybe it's her."

"Excuse me, ma'am," Carson said to the woman with the newspaper. "Do you mind if we copy down the address from that ad?"

The waitress glanced over. "Oh, Sarah Monk? She's my stylist. Does my color every six weeks. Bet you couldn't even tell I wasn't a real blonde."

"I wouldn't have been able to tell," Olivia said, which was true. The color was very natural and soft. And Olivia liked the cut, kind of a long bob with bangs.

"She's the best," the waitress said, refilling their coffees. "I just love Sarah. And those green eyes of hers. Stunning. Tell her Lorraine sent you. Maybe she'll give me a discount on my color next time."

Those green eyes. Olivia and Carson locked gazes. He quickly jotted down the address of the salon, placed a ten-dollar bill on the counter, thanked the waitress and then they ran to his car.

"Leeville is just two towns over. A small town, not much there."

"Except maybe my aunt!" Olivia said, excitement building.

Fifteen minutes later, they'd arrived at Style Mile. The salon was between an apartment building and a real estate office. When they walked in, a woman with very green eyes stood up and put down her magazine. "Hi, how can I help you?"

"We heard Sarah Monk is working here now and does great work," Carson said.

Please don't say you're Sarah, Olivia thought. *Say that Sarah Monk of the stunning green eyes is in the back and will be right with you. And then Aunt Sarah will walk out, see me and run over and hug me. I'll have my aunt back.*

Please, please, please.

"I'm Sarah Monk," she said, and Olivia's heart plummeted.

"Sorry," Carson whispered to Olivia. "Um, we'll be back another time. My friend isn't feeling well."

She *wasn't* feeling well. At all. They were never going to find Sarah.

He led Olivia outside and wrapped her in a hug so warm and enveloping that she let herself droop against his strength. "I know it's disappointing. But I made you a promise that we'll find her, and we will."

She took in a breath and let it out. "I guess it'll just take time. You said you had a lead here about your young client's dad. Maybe we should turn our attention to that case."

He looked at her for a moment, as if making sure she was really okay. "We've hit all the salons in Stockton, so that's two more towns crossed off the list. I do like the notion of sticking close to rodeo or ranching towns. I have a good idea where to focus the search next."

She nodded. "So where to now for your young client?"

"His mom said we'd likely find her ex-husband either working the rodeo as a hand or at one of the ranches nearby. That's what he did for a living before they got married and he started drinking and got fired, leaving his ex to support the family. I called ahead to the rodeo and there are three Steve Johnsons working as hands. The manager I spoke to said the hands who don't have their own places bunk near the barns."

"Seems hard to imagine a man leaving his family to go live in a bunkhouse," Olivia said.

"I know."

Minutes later they were back in Carson's SUV and driving over to the rodeo. There weren't any events going on right now, so the place was pretty deserted except for employees. Carson parked and they wound their way over to the barns and walked through the field. When they passed a couple men, Carson asked if they knew "a Steve Johnson, late twenties," and one of the guys pointed to a man washing down a bull up ahead. Carson checked his phone, sliding through photos. Olivia could see it was the same guy.

"Are you going to talk to him?" she asked.

He shook his head. "My job is to find him. I need to let my client know I've done so, and then we can talk about next steps. If I go up to Johnson and introduce myself and let him know his son hired me to find him, that he just wants to see him, Johnson may bolt. I can't risk that."

Olivia nodded, her heart heavy. She crossed her arms over her chest as they walked back to his car, suddenly cold despite the warm afternoon.

"You okay?" he said as he opened her car door for her.

"I'm glad you found him and that it was easier than finding my aunt has been. I'm happy for your nine-year-old client. I guess I'm thinking about my own dad," she admitted. "My mother told him she was pregnant with his child, and he was gone the next day, never seen or heard from again. I've always known not to take it personally—I mean, it's not like he knew me, right? But still. I had a father for that space of time and he chose not to take on that title. I just don't get it."

"I don't get it, either, Liv," he said, and she was struck by the nickname, that he felt close enough to her to use it. "My dad didn't leave us but he certainly wasn't part of the family. I never got that, either. I can't imagine not being there for Danny, being very present and active in his life."

"Good," she said, reaching up and touching his shoulder, his navy blue Henley shirt warm from the sun.

He put his hand over hers and tilted her chin up with his finger and then kissed her. She closed her eyes, losing herself in how sweet it felt, how good. Her knees felt slightly shaky and she held on to him, wanting to stay in his arms forever.

But his phone rang.

"Blasted timing," he said, smiling at her. He glanced at the phone. "My dad. He's watching Danny so I'd better take this." He answered the call and listened for a minute, then explained to Olivia that his dad said he took Danny out for gelato at the new place that opened in Oak Creek and there was a hair salon right next to it. A stylist with auburn hair, green eyes and a tattoo on her arm was blow-drying someone's hair right by the window. "Does your aunt have a tattoo on her arm?"

"She didn't back then, but she might have gotten one."

"Dad," he said into the phone, "why not just go inside and ask her if her name is Sarah?" He listened for a moment. "Okay. We're on our way." He put down the phone and turned to Olivia. "Looks like we're going to Oak Creek to see if this woman is your aunt," Carson said. "For some reason, my dad doesn't want to ask her himself. I'm not sure what's going on with him."

Edmund Ford hadn't wanted to see a photo of Sarah Mack, though Olivia had offered to show him one. He'd said he wanted to be surprised, that he didn't need to know what she looked like until he laid eyes on her for the first time, that he'd feel something in his heart the moment he saw his Sarah and that was all he needed to go on.

"Case of the nerves, maybe?" Olivia said. "It could very well be her. Right next door to where we grew up."

Olivia's hope was back.

It took an hour, but they finally arrived in Oak Creek. Carson's dad had taken Danny to the playground in the interim and the plan was to meet back at the bench in front of the salon at 4:15 p.m. Edmund and Danny hadn't arrived yet.

Carson peered in the big bay window of the salon, Delia's Hair and Day Spa, but the glare from the sun made it difficult to see inside.

"This is one of the most expensive salons in the area," Olivia said. "But surely your dad called here when he first began his search, if not visited for one of his seven haircuts. And you said you called all the local salons to ask if any Sarahs worked there."

"Your aunt may have changed her name entirely. Maybe that's why she's been so hard to find. And who knows—maybe this stylist he noticed today wasn't working the day he came in to see if anyone matched the description."

Because of the setting sun and the glare likely streaming inside, the shades lining the windows had been lowered, but Carson could see a tanned arm with many silver bangle bracelets moving and a hand wielding a blow-dryer, while a woman sat in a big silver chair.

"Dada!"

Carson glanced left and there was Danny on his dad's shoulders as they headed toward the bench.

"That's the second time today I've seen Danny on the shoulders of a Ford," Olivia said to Carson, smiling at the pair as they approached.

"Hi, Liva!" Danny said, holding out his arms.

Carson glanced at Olivia, whose expression told him that her heart had just melted into a puddle. Danny had that effect on people.

Edmund effortlessly lifted Danny off his shoulders and handed him to Olivia, who scooped him into a hug.

"Meat song!" Danny said.

Olivia laughed. "How about one verse now and then the rest on the way home?"

"Top 'getty," Danny sang and started to giggle.

Now it was Carson's turn to laugh. Olivia sat down on the bench, Danny cuddled close against her chest, and she started to sing-whisper about a meatball all covered in cheese.

"Okay, now we have to go see something inside this place," she told Danny, "but after, I'm going to sing the rest and you can help me sing it."

"Cheese!" Danny sang.

Olivia laughed and stood back up, Danny in her arms. "Edmund, may I ask why you didn't want to go in and ask her name?"

Edmund took a breath and let it out. "Because… well, I did go in and I looked right at her and she does have lovely green eyes. But—" He stopped, as if weighing something, thinking something over.

"But what, Dad?" Carson asked.

"I looked right at that woman with her auburn hair and her green eyes and her tattoo and I didn't feel a thing," he said, disappointment clouding his features. "Madam Miranda told me that when I see my Sarah, I'd know it. I didn't know anything when I looked at this stylist. I didn't feel anything at all."

Carson could have done a cartwheel. "Dad, *of course* you didn't feel anything. Why would you feel the earth move and your heart start beating like a teenager over a total stranger? Like I've been telling you for weeks now, it's all just make-believe. Nice to hear but with no basis in reality."

His father's expression—and Olivia's—told him he might have gone a little too far. Dammit.

"Dad, I just mean that you get your life back," he said quickly. "Olivia gets her aunt back. Everything goes back to normal."

"Normal?" Edmund repeated, glaring at Carson. "How dare you," he added on a harsh whisper, mindful of his grandson. "I like my prediction. And I intend to see it fulfilled. With or without you."

Olivia stepped forward, Danny in her arms, the boy looking from his father to his grandfather. "Why don't we go in," she said to Carson. "And see if it's my aunt." Olivia reached out her arms to transfer Danny to his grandfather, whose expression softened the moment he held the boy. "Danny, I can't wait to sing you the rest of the song! Your dad and I are going to go inside this shop but we'll be back in a minute."

Edmund turned away and began pointing to cars. "What color is that one, Danny?"

"Blue!" Danny said.

"Dad, I—" Carson began. But what was he going to say? If it was Sarah Mack inside, she *would* be just a stranger to Edmund. Was his father really expecting to be shot with Cupid's arrow and to fall instantly in love? How could his dad really put so much stock in a fortune? Carson didn't get it.

His father didn't even turn back around. He held up a hand in Carson's direction, then faced Olivia. "Please let me know if it's your aunt."

"I will," she said, shooting Carson a death glare before walking up the three steps to the front door of the salon.

As they entered, he *felt* Olivia's frown, felt her entire body turn inward, which meant the stylist was not her aunt. But she was a green-eyed hairstylist—that he could see with his own eyes—and her name *was* Sarah, evident from the engraved silver name tag pinned to her sleek black bolero jacket. She had three visible tattoos, wrist, arm and a small one behind the left ear, a starfish, if he was seeing correctly at this slight distance. She could easily have another on her ankle, which was covered by shiny black glued-on pants.

"She's not my aunt," Olivia whispered, "but I didn't think she would be."

Carson stared at her. "Because the moment my father does encounter your aunt, you expect him to have hearts shooting out of his chest like the love-struck raccoon on the cartoon Danny watches?"

She crossed her arms over her chest. "It doesn't matter anyway. She's not my aunt."

"Your mother never told my father that the Sarah of his prediction was your aunt. Just that she was a green-eyed hairstylist named Sarah with a particular tattoo. Since that tattoo is of common symbols of the trade, this very woman herself might have that same tattoo. Your mother might not have been talking about her sister at all. This woman *could* be my father's predicted bride."

She shook her head as though that was ridiculous. "Carson, come on."

"Excuse me," Carson said to the stylist. "We're looking for a specific stylist who works here named Sarah, but we were told she'd have a tattoo on her ankle of a blow-dryer and brush."

The woman smiled. "That's me." She leaned down and began lifting the hem of her pants on her left leg.

Victory! Yes! This was the predicted green-eyed hairstylist named Sarah with the tattoo. And his father felt zippo, nothing, nada! It was all a dumb little game and it was over. His father would be disappointed, sure, but now that he knew he did want love in his life, he could look for someone he liked—instead of someone a "fortune-teller" *told* him he'd like.

"I think we're done here," Carson whispered to Olivia. But as the stylist continued to roll up her pants, a tattoo taking up half her calf began to reveal itself of black blow-dryer and a black brush. Shoot. Dammit. "What color did you say that blow-dryer and brush were?" he added to Olivia.

"The blow-dryer is hot pink and the brush is silver," Olivia said. "And the tattoo is very small and just above the ankle bone."

"Guess I'm not your Sarah then," the woman said and went back to blow-drying her customer.

He was glum. Olivia was glum.

And through the door, he could see that his father had Danny up on his shoulders and was pointing out the different kinds of cars that were parked.

Instead of waiting with bated breath for them to come out, to learn if the woman was his predicted great love, his dad was focused on Danny. That was the man he'd become.

Suddenly Carson felt terrible about hoping to disappoint his father, about hoping this woman he felt nothing for, had no attraction to, would be his predicted great love.

What the hell was wrong with him? Was this the kind of father *he* wanted to be?

Dammit, dammit, dammit.

"Well, what's the verdict?" Edmund asked as Carson stepped outside. "From your expression, Carson, I'm hopeful that she's Olivia's aunt. You look…disappointed."

Knife. Twist. "She's not Olivia's aunt," he said. "She's not your predicted second great love."

He watched relief cross his father's features, and then realization of some kind that Carson must have turned some figurative corner about the whole thing. He hadn't, not about the prediction and fortune-telling.

"I do want you to be happy, Dad," he said.

Edmund clapped him on the back. "I'm glad to hear that."

So why did Carson feel so…conflicted? What was burning in his gut? Something didn't feel right. Something felt very wrong.

Olivia finally came down the stairs, disappointment etched on her face, and he wanted to scoop her up into his arms and assure her again that they'd find Sarah Mack. As he took a step toward her, Danny said, "Liva!"

Olivia's entire face brightened. She rushed down the steps to Danny and beamed at him.

His dad put Carson's son before his own feelings. Olivia put his son before her own feelings.

It was time for Carson to start putting others before his own cynical heart.

But the more he watched Olivia sing the meatball song and then one about an itsy-bitsy spider as she made spiders out of her fingers, the more he realized this was all going to be over be soon and she'd be out of their lives.

He always put Danny before himself. Which meant saving Danny from another woman in his life walking away. Once Carson found Sarah Mack, Olivia would go her way, Carson would go his.

Except if her aunt was really her father's predicted love, Sarah Mack would be part of their lives. Which meant Olivia would be, too.

Suddenly this was getting more complicated. Either

way, someone was going to get hurt, and he wasn't sure who.

His phone rang. The Blue Gulch PD, who often hired him to help out on cases.

"Carson, this is Detective Nick Slater. You asked me to let you know if a Sarah Mack came up in the system. I was just looking for leads on a suspect and I noticed a woman named Sarah Mack was stopped for a traffic violation on Blue Gulch Street at three o'clock today."

Huh. "Date of birth and address?"

Slater read off the information. The DOB matched the right age for Olivia's aunt. And even if she went by a different name professionally, the name Sarah Mack was on her license. Unfortunately, the address on the license was her old place in Blue Gulch; she clearly didn't live in Blue Gulch anymore.

"What was the violation? Speeding?" Carson asked.

"Actually, she was going too slow. Five miles per hour in a thirty zone. She had people honking at her. She was let go with a warning."

"I owe you one, Detective Slater. Thanks."

"You've done so much for the Blue Gulch PD. It's my pleasure to help you out." Slater was married to one of the Hurleys of Hurley's Homestyle Kitchen, the family who owned the food truck that Olivia worked in.

After getting the make, model and year of the car, plus the plate number, Carson put his phone away. He looked at Olivia, now singing a different song to Danny a few feet away on the bench in front of the salon.

He was afraid to get her hopes up again. But he had a feeling that he would be reuniting Olivia with her aunt today.

If Sarah Mack was still in Blue Gulch, the car would

be easy to spot. Not many old yellow VW Beetles on the road these days. If she'd come and gone, that was another story. But it was just a matter of time—not if.

"Hey, you two," Carson said, heading over. "I've got some news you're both gonna like."

Chapter Eight

Olivia felt it in her bones; she would be seeing her aunt very soon. She just knew it. But as quickly as the good feeling had come, it faded to nothing. She shivered inside Carson's SUV despite the unusually warm February day.

Edmund had taken a sleepy Danny back to his house for a nap, and Olivia and Carson headed over to Blue Gulch to search Blue Gulch Street and the one hotel and B and B for a yellow VW bug. Her aunt hadn't had that car when she lived in Blue Gulch, but the style of car sounded like something her aunt would like.

"The traffic stop was two hours ago?" Olivia asked, craning her neck to look for the car as Carson turned onto Blue Gulch Street, the main drag of town where the shops and restaurants were, including the Hurley's Homestyle Kitchen food truck. "I wonder if she's still in town. Maybe she just passed through." Huh. Maybe she wouldn't be seeing her aunt so soon, after all.

"There's only reason someone goes five miles an hour on the main road in town," Carson said. "Because she's looking for someone on the street or for someone in store windows."

"You think my aunt was looking for me? Why not call? Why not come by? Why not leave a note in the mailbox?"

"Maybe she just looks for you," he said. "Maybe she drives through Blue Gulch often, hoping to spot you, just get a glimpse of you."

"But that would mean she still cares about me," Olivia said.

"I'm sure she does care. Sometimes, people leave your life for reasons that have nothing to do with you. They're consumed by something else and it drives them away."

"Like your nine-year-old client's father, most likely," she said.

"Exactly. I always say I don't get it, but I guess I do. I mean, I understand, intellectually, why some people walk out on their lives and families. But I'll never get it emotionally."

She nodded. "You look left, I'll look right." But nowhere that she could see, on the street or parked in the spots, was a yellow Beetle.

"You have no idea at all what caused the estrangement between your mother and aunt?" Carson asked.

They passed the library and the coffee shop and the food truck, which had a nice line. Olivia scanned the parking lot by the town green. No yellow Beetle.

"I know that my aunt never wanted to talk about

fortune-telling or the family 'gifts' and that there was a secret. I'm not sure whose—my mother's or my aunt's. I once heard the tail end of an argument and my aunt saying, 'Don't you ever bring them up again,' but that was the last I heard of that and when I asked my mother what 'them' referred to, she just waved her hand dismissively. Three weeks later, my aunt sold her house, which I discovered because of the sold sign on the lawn and she was gone. No goodbye. Nothing. That was five years ago. My mother wouldn't talk about it or speculate. I finally stopped asking."

"The argument must have been about something important to drive your aunt away," he said gently.

"I know. I just have no idea what it involved. When my mother got sick, I started looking for my aunt but couldn't find her. I was sure Sarah would want to know, to be there to make amends. And in the days before the funeral, I doubled my efforts to find her. Having that to focus on was the only thing that kept me from falling apart. But I didn't find her. She doesn't even know her sister is gone." Olivia burst into tears, unable to help herself or stop herself. She covered her face in her hands and sobbed.

Carson parked the car and drew her into his arms. She resisted at first, miserable, sad, tears falling down her cheeks, but then she gave in to the comfort and held on to him, gave in to depth of her sadness. The loss of her aunt, the loss of her mother, the loss of the father she never knew. Hell, she was even crying for Danny and the loss of his mother. For Carson's young client, and the loss of his father.

She felt him put his head down on top of hers, resting his cheek as he stroked her hair, one hand tight around her shoulders.

"You've lost a lot, Olivia, but you're about to *find*," Carson said, tipping up her chin.

She looked into his hazel-green eyes and felt better, stronger. "I'm mortified that I just started blubbering."

"Don't be," he said. "Best way to deal with strong emotions is to let 'em rip."

"Well, thanks for letting me literally cry on your shoulder."

He leaned forward, taking her face in his hand, and kissed her, wiping away the tears under her eyes. Then he dropped his hands to his lap and turned to face forward. "I've got to stop doing that."

"Or keep doing that," she said.

"Olivia, I'm not…"

"Looking for romance. So you said. Yet you keep kissing me. Interesting."

He smiled, then laughed. "I just don't want to mess up here, Olivia. You're a good, kind person and I don't want to hurt you."

He was guarded, but she was a grown-up and either she'd bust through those walls of his or she wouldn't. *Love would out*, as they said. Or it wouldn't.

Feeling better and stronger, Olivia sat up straight. "Let's drive past the hotel and B and B, and check for my aunt's car," she said, deftly changing the subject.

The car wasn't at the hotel in the center of Blue Gulch Street or at the B and B on a side street near Olivia's house. Carson did another drive-by of the main road, but they didn't see the yellow Beetle.

"That she was here is a sign that she's ready to come out of hiding," Carson said. "Do you think she knows you're looking for her? If she has the family gift or whatever."

She glanced at him. *That* was a sign that he didn't find it as far-fetched as he had before. "It's possible. She wouldn't talk about her gift. I don't know what it is or even if she has one. And my mother would never talk about it."

"Well, maybe she senses you're looking for her and she came to town today to see if she'd run in to you."

Olivia shrugged. "She knows where I live."

"The two of you will reunite. That I do believe," he said, giving her hand a squeeze. "I'll take you home. It's been quite a day."

It had been. She squeezed his hand back, missing the warmth and strength of it as he put it on the wheel.

Olivia's mother's face came to mind. She wished Madam Miranda was here to tell her whether she was setting herself up for a broken heart.

An hour later, Carson was sitting in the Johnson living room, his nine-year-old client, Joey, sitting straight up on the sofa next to his mother, whom Carson had called earlier after dropping off Olivia at her house. He'd let Tara Johnson know he had located her ex-husband at the rodeo, where he worked as a ranch hand. They'd made arrangements for Carson to stop by at six o'clock.

"I didn't say anything to your father," Carson said to Joey. "He doesn't know that you hired me or that you're looking for him. I wanted to locate him first and let you know where he is so that you can decide how you want to handle the next steps."

"My mom and I talked about it," Joey said, brushing his long, sandy blond bangs away from his eyes. "If you're willing, will you come with me to talk to him?"

Carson hadn't been expecting that.

"It just seems more official if the private investigator I hired to find him is there, you know?" Joey explained. "I feel like he'd more willing to tell the truth. I don't know."

"Well, I'm happy to take you to see him, if that's okay with your mom."

"It's fine with me," Tara Johnson said. "And I appreciate what you've done for Joey. It's a hard situation. My only concern is Joey's feelings. You can tell his dad that I'm not looking for him to haul him into court or anything like that. I know he has problems. I know he has no money. I know he's probably working for room and board. I only care that Joey has a relationship with his dad."

Tears glistened in Joey's eyes and he leaned his head against his mother's arm. Hell, now Carson felt a tear poking at his own eyes. "I did find out his work schedule for the week," Carson said. "If you want to go after school or on the weekend, he works then. We can catch him just as his shift is ending so he'll be free to talk."

They arranged to go in two days, when Joey's school had a half day and he didn't have baseball practice.

"You're a brave kid," he said to Joey as the boy walked him to the door. "I had some issues with my dad but I was always too bottled up inside to confront him. I admire you."

The boy looked up at Carson with such open brown eyes that it took everything in him not to hug him tight. He put out his hand and Joey shook it. "See you in a couple days."

"Thanks for finding him," Joey said. "If you want to

know a secret," he added on a whisper, "I'm just glad he's alive. I wasn't sure if you'd come back and say he wasn't. My mom warned me about that."

"I know what you mean," Carson said.

Outside, on the doorstep, he couldn't help wondering if Danny would be having a conversation like this some day. Wondering where his mother was, if she was still alive, *why* the big question. Heavyhearted, he got into his car. He couldn't get home to hug his son soon enough.

The next morning, Dory was helping out in the food truck since there was a sidewalk sale on Blue Gulch Street and people would be out in droves. Olivia had done a lot of the prep work this morning, but even with Dory taking orders and dealing with the cash register and Olivia cooking, Olivia still only had two hands for cooking.

While she was sautéing shrimp, she couldn't help but notice that Amanda Buckman, harried mom of twin four-year-old boys and twin eight-year-old girls, had just bites left of her eggplant-parm po'boy and her expression and body language had changed. Where before she'd been slumped and tired-looking, she now sat up straight, her face tilted to the sun, and she smiled at her daughters doing cartwheels on the green while the boys finished their kid-size chicken-finger po'boys and swung their legs. Miles Fincello, the pharmacist at the drugstore, who'd ordered a pulled-pork po'boy with extra barbecue sauce and a mini vanilla-cream cannoli with pistachios, had come to the window with worry etched on his face; now, he was chatting on his cell phone, smiling. And Molly Euling, whose house was on the corner of Blue Gulch Street and Golden Way, Olivia's street, and was always snapping at dog walkers to keep their "mutts" off her grass, was now petting the loud pug she was always complaining about.

A good day's work—regarding both Olivia's special ability and sales. The Hurleys would be very pleased with the day's receipts, that was for sure.

"Pardon me, excuse me, excuse me," a loud voice said at the food truck window. "Dory, smile for me, will you?"

"May I help you?" Dory said to the pushy man who Olivia didn't recognize.

"I'm Hal Herbert from the *Blue Gulch County Gazette*. I'd like to get a few shots of you for the paper and our website. Can you hold the order pad a bit higher so it can make the frame?"

"Why on earth would you want to get pictures of me taking orders in the Hurley Homestyle Kitchen food truck?" Dory asked. "I'm just helping out a friend."

"Just doing my job, miss," the man said. "There's going to be a feature on Beaufort Harrington." He consulted his own little notebook. "Your fiancé. Apparently he's throwing his hat into the Blue Gulch mayoral race." The guy took a couple more pictures, then scribbled something in the notebook.

"Yes, I know that," Dory said. "But why are the newspapers so interested in *me* and *my* life?" she asked, looking at Olivia in confusion. "This morning, when I was up early at the bakery to get the breads done, another reporter stopped by to take pictures of me sliding the loaves in the oven. I didn't even have time to get the flour off my face."

"I guess that's the world of politics," Olivia said. "Maybe candidates' brides-to-be sell papers?"

Dory shrugged. "How did you know I'd be here, anyway?" she asked the reporter.

The man consulted his notebook. "Looks like a Mrs. Harrington has been calling in your schedule."

"Annalee?" Dory said after the man had taken more pictures and gone. "Olivia, why is Annalee Harrington so interested in having photos of me working here and at the bakery in the paper? And did you see the captions of the photos from the engagement toast gathering? My mother's 'dime-store' earrings? I was so angry about that jab."

"Maybe you should talk to Beaufort about what's going on," Olivia said.

"I absolutely will." She glanced out the window. "Oh, the gals from the library are heading our way. And a bunch of teachers from the middle school, too."

"I'm ready!" Olivia said.

Olivia got back to work, but she couldn't help peering out the window of the food truck, looking for two people in particular.

Carson, who was a no-show, and whose handsome face she missed.

And her aunt. She supposed it was silly to think Sarah would just walk up to the food truck and say, "Oh, hi, Olivia, it's your aunt" after five years of radio silence. But if she'd been around yesterday, maybe she would do just that. Maybe Sarah was ready to talk again. If so, where was she? Olivia had stayed up past midnight expecting the doorbell to ring, her aunt to be on the other side. But the doorbell hadn't rung once.

Olivia turned her attention back to the stove and

sauté pans. She had five orders of the special po'boy of the day, a scrumptious meat loaf, if she did say so herself, and seven other kinds to make, plus a bunch of cannoli.

She had wrapped up the final tuna-melt po'boy when she heard a sharp voice say, "Dory, you don't need to work here."

Olivia glanced past Dory's shoulder to see her fiancé, Beaufort Harrington, standing there with some of his coworkers from Texas Trust. Edmund Ford was not among them.

"Dory, you're my fiancé. You don't have to work at all. You know that. You don't even have to work in the bakery—you can hire someone to manage the place for you and all the extra employees you need. You're going to be a Harrington, for God's sake."

"I'm helping out my friend Olivia," Dory said. "I told you about Olivia Mack. I've been her assistant with her catering business in the past."

"Sweetheart, there's no need to assist anyone," Beaufort said.

"Let's talk about this later," Dory told him. "There's quite a line, as you can see."

Beaufort ordered a shrimp po'boy. He didn't look happy.

Olivia wondered what would happen to Beaufort's mood after he ate the po'boy she was making for him. She spread on the remoulade, layered the shrimp and wrapped it up.

As the line died down now that it was past two, she kept an eye on Beaufort Harrington. He finished the po'boy, stood up and came back over to the truck.

"Dory, I just meant that you're going to be my wife.

You don't need to work. You're going to have a lot of social engagements, especially once my candidacy is officially announced."

If her po'boy had any effect on Beaufort it was to make him more emphatic about Dory *not* working.

"Beau, why would your mother send reporters to take pictures of me working at the bakery and here, then?"

Beaufort's cheeks turned pink. "Oh, you know my mother."

"What do you mean?" she asked.

"Gotta run, sweetheart. See you later. Great po'boy, Olivia," he called out. Then he hurried away.

"What do you think is going on with Annalee Harrington?" Dory asked.

"I don't know. But it looks like you and Beaufort have a lot to iron out before you get married. You've made it pretty clear you intend to run the bakery yourself, not hire someone to keep it going."

Dory nodded. "I have made that clear. Maybe Beaufort thinks I'm more interested in the money than the shop. But he's wrong."

"I think you two just need to talk. If this is primarily a business arrangement, the business has to be ironed out."

Dory brightened. "You're right." She glanced at Olivia. "Hey, I know you just made a thousand po'boys, but before you put away the ham, can you make me a good old-fashioned ham-and-cheese with your amazing honey mustard? No one makes a po'boy like you."

"Of course," Olivia said.

As Olivia made one last sandwich and Dory helped her clean up and get the truck ready for the dinner shift that Dylan would be taking over, Olivia had a bad feeling that things with Beaufort might not go as Dory had thought.

She watched Dory eat the po'boy, her friend's shoulders rising, her chin lifting. Dory's eyes narrowed. She took the final bite of the sandwich and nodded to herself as if making some kind of decision.

"Olivia, I've got to run. I have someone to see before closing time."

Hmm. Just what had she infused Dory's sandwich with?

Chapter Nine

After making dinner for himself and Danny, Carson settled the toddler in his car seat and hit the road to Blue Gulch to look for Sarah Mack's car. No sign of it. He did see his dad walking and window-shopping, a bag from Blue Gulch Toys on his arm. He pulled over and surprised Edmund Ford. The look on his father's face at the sight of Danny never failed to stop Carson in his tracks. Pure love, thrill, delight. The way a parent's face should light up. Danny was overjoyed by the stuffed panda Grandpa had picked up for him.

Carson's phone rang—Beaufort Harrington. The man could barely speak.

"I wanted you to hear it from me instead of the local press or gossips," Beaufort spluttered, his voice broken. "Dory called off the engagement. One minute we're engaged and the next we're not. I saw her just a couple hours ago at the Hurley's food truck—she was helping out the woman who runs it. And suddenly an hour later, she hands me back my ring."

He froze. The food truck. Olivia. Had her "ability" somehow interfered?

Come on. That would be crazy. She made po'boys and cannoli. She didn't have special abilities to "lift hearts" or break them with her food. She was just a good cook and people liked to eat. Add those together and you got smiles. End of story. Whatever had happened between Dory and Beaufort had nothing to do with Olivia or the food truck. "Oh, man," Carson said. "I'm really sorry."

"Me, too. My parents are here now—I'd better go. Talk to you soon."

What the heck happened?

He let his dad know what was going on and took Edmund up on his offer to bring Danny home and put him to bed so that he could talk to Olivia. Beaufort was an old friend, and to hear him so torn up was heartbreaking. And something told him there was more to the story than anyone knew.

Olivia had spent a long morning and afternoon at the food truck. After her shift she made Mr. Crenshaw chicken Milanese with a side of fettuccine in light cream sauce and delivered it, sitting awhile with him to catch up on his romance with widow Eleanor Parkerton who lived one floor up. Then she'd made another client's Weight Watchers–friendly meal of exactly eight points, delivered that and finally was curled up with Sweetie on the divan in her mother's fortune-telling parlor, looking through family photos.

Aunt Sarah on a bicycle, her auburn hair blowing back in the wind, a joyful smile on her face. Her mother with the enigmatic expression in her eyes as she sat on the porch of their house, Sweetie in her lap. Their grandmother, also a fortune-teller, a woman Olivia hadn't had the chance to know, with her two daughters as teenagers. And one of Olivia's father, the only photo there was of him in the album. She stared at it, always surprised to see a bit of herself in the man's face, as though she should look nothing like the stranger he was. She used to think about seeking him out, but decided against it long ago. He'd left before she was born, and Olivia didn't even know his last name. Her mother had told her that the man had been utterly irresistible to her. Even though she knew he'd break her heart and she'd never see him again, she thought she could use her strong will to conquer what would happen. Miranda had told Olivia she wouldn't have willingly gotten pregnant knowing the father of her baby wouldn't stick around; she *would* have resisted him and not have had their short-lived few weeks together. But all Miranda's attempts to keep him in her life had failed, and Madam Miranda had further accepted that she couldn't rewrite the truth, no matter how badly she wanted to.

Olivia didn't like any of that. What the hell was the point of anything, then, if you couldn't write your own destiny, be the captain of your own ship? She pressed her face against Sweetie's fur, the old cat's purring a comfort. Sometimes she believed what her mother had—that life had a plan for you and all the little detours were part of that plan. The things-happen-for-a-reason point of view. And sometimes she was like

Carson—pragmatic, logical, about the here and now and what made sense. The you-decide team. Carson would say that if her mother had supposedly known Olivia's father wouldn't stick around, then she could have chosen not to sleep with him and create a life. But she had anyway and, oh, look! Then again, Carson seemed to be coming around—slowly—to the idea that her mother *may* have had special abilities.

What Olivia believed was this: her mother had fallen in love, had known it was doomed, but also had known there would be a daughter who she would love more than anything. In a way, her mother had both broken her own heart and healed it.

"I don't know, Sweetie," she said to the cat, giving her a scratch on the head and taking a sip of her tea.

The doorbell rang, startling Olivia. She went to the front door to find Dory standing there.

"Dory, is everything okay?"

Before Dory could answer, a black SUV pulled up to the house. Carson.

He came up to the door and saw Dory. Looking a bit uncomfortable he said, "Sorry to interrupt. To be honest, I just got a call from Beaufort and he's pretty broken up." He turned to walk back down the porch steps. "I'll let you two talk."

"No," Dory said to Carson. "I know you're a good friend of Beaufort's and close with Olivia. And I know Olivia won't feel comfortable breaking a confidence and telling you what I told her, so I'll tell you myself."

"Come into the living room, both of you," Olivia said. She led the way and gestured for Dory and Carson to sit. Carson chose one end of the sofa; Dory sat on the chair across from it. Olivia bit her lip and sat next to Carson.

"Carson, what you might not know," Dory began, "is that the reason I accepted Beaufort's marriage proposal after dating such a short time was because he offered to save my family business, Drummond's Bake Shop. My mother died recently and her bills took my accounts. There's nothing left and the shop is next to go. But Beaufort said he would save the shop if I married him."

"I'm very sorry about your mother, Dory," Carson said. "To have your family business in jeopardy on top of a such a loss must be very painful and very difficult."

Olivia found herself reaching over to touch Carson's hand. That was a kind thing to say.

Dory nodded, the sadness in her blue eyes heartbreaking. "Tonight I found out why Beaufort proposed. It was part of a whole plan to present me as his wife from the wrong side of the tracks, so that he'd look less privileged and more accepting, more like a regular guy instead of a wealthy one-percenter type. His 'people' wanted him to have a wife with a certain look—petite, blonde, nonthreatening with a good backstory. Who knew my growing-up in the Blue Gulch trailer park would be so appealing to a future politician?"

Carson frowned. "That doesn't sound like Beaufort."

Olivia didn't know Beaufort Harrington well, if at all, but he'd always seemed like a follower rather than a leader. Perhaps his mother was behind all the plans. Based on the news articles and photos, Olivia wouldn't doubt it.

"Well, he has his ambitions," Dory said. "And I can't fault him for picking and choosing his wife based on all that when I said yes so that my family business would be saved."

"But now your family business won't be saved," Olivia said. "What are you going to do?"

Dory pulled a folder from her tote bag. "My hopes are in here. A business plan. Six months ago, when I saw the writing on the wall about the bakery, I presented a plan to my bank for a loan and was turned down. But after seeing how you and the Hurleys run the food truck, why it's so successful, I have new ideas. I wrote up a new plan tonight and I'm going to present it to my bank tomorrow. I have a good feeling about it."

Whether Olivia's ham-and-cheese po'boy with honey mustard helped spur Dory to rely on herself or whether Dory just realized what she really wanted and needed, Olivia was happy for her friend.

"In any case, Olivia, your mother was right. I don't love Beaufort. You know what I do love? My bakery. I need to do this myself. I'm going to save Drummond's Bake Shop." She stood and stopped for a moment to pet Sweetie, who was weaving between her legs, then headed for the door.

"Good for you, Dory," Olivia said, hugging her friend.

"Best of luck to you with the shop and the loan," Carson said.

Dory smiled and left, and Carson narrowed his eyes at Olivia.

"So your mother was the one who put it in her head not to marry Beaufort?" The frown was back.

"Carson, that's the least of what happened. Dory

doesn't love Beaufort. Beaufort doesn't love her. A marriage based on a deal has been canceled. That's all."

He leaned back on the couch. "So we have people making important decisions with legal and lifelong significance based on a fortune-teller's prediction. We have people making decisions based on necessity. What the hell ever happened to getting married because you fell in love?"

Olivia sat down beside Carson. "I'm holding out for that."

"I should hope so," he said, crossing his arms over his chest.

"Huh," Olivia said. "So you do have faith, after all."

He frowned. "Faith? What are you talking about?"

"You do believe in love."

"I believe in marrying for the right reason," he said. "The right reason is love. That doesn't mean I believe in love anymore. I don't. I used to, but not anymore."

"You love Danny. You love your dad." *I wish I could add myself to that list*, Olivia realized, her heart clenching.

"I believe in facts. I believe in people walking the walk. My son has my unconditional love—you bet he does. My father changed. He earned my respect back. He earned my love back."

Olivia glanced at him, the hard set of his jaw, the flash of intensity in his eyes.

"When my son was so frail in the NICU at birth and the doctors weren't sure he'd make it, I kept caressing his tiny fingers through those window holes in his incubator and thinking over and over if only his mother were still there, Danny would know it, he'd feel her there, feel her love, and he'd get better. I thought the reason he was getting worse was because he knew his mother had given up on him and walked out."

Oh, Carson. She bit her lip and wanted to put her arms around him, but he looked like he might bolt at any moment so she stayed quiet. This was a time to listen, not talk.

"But you know what happened?" he said, turning to face her. "Danny did start getting better. Because I was there, because his grandfather was there. Because of the fantastic nurses and doctors. He got better and I realized his mother being around or not had nothing to do with it. He'd be fine. And so would I."

She got it now. This wasn't about faith or love or lack thereof regarding either or both. This was about Carson Ford's refusal to let himself need anyone or anything.

"When my ex-wife was pregnant," Carson said, "she had her fortune told at a carnival in Oak Creek. For ten bucks she was told she'd have a daughter who would be perfect and look just like her. Jodie ran around buying pink layettes and nursery decorations. Instead, our *son* was born eight weeks early and sickly and looked exactly like me. I don't think Jodie ever got over the 'betrayal.'" He shook his head. "I loved Jodie, but after that it was easy to let go of the love."

"I can understand that," she said, reaching over to squeeze his hand. And now she knew a bit more why her mother's profession and his father being involved with a fortune-teller affected him the way it did.

"Tell me something, Olivia. Why didn't your mother tell you who *your* great love would be?"

Talk about a change of subject. A subject she didn't want to discuss—not with Carson. Not with the man she loved. Olivia glanced away. "She must have had her reasons. She did tell me my last boyfriend wasn't the one. And he wasn't."

"Self-fulfilling prophecy? You dumped him?"

"He fell in love with someone else and proposed, like, a day later," she said, wincing at the memory. "That was the end of us."

"I think your mother never told you who your great love is because she had no idea. The way it should be. No knows these things in advance. My dad will find that out when we finally find your aunt."

"I think my mother did know," Olivia said slowly, testing out the words on her heart. Could Carson be the one? Her great love? If he was, he sure was making it difficult. "There was no need to tell me who. No need to lead."

"Like your mother did with my father," he muttered. "She *led* him right to your aunt. And now look how close we are to finding her. A total setup. I'm still not sure what all that means, Olivia. But I know you're a very honest, good person. And from everything I've learned about Madam Miranda, she was, too."

Olivia nodded, appreciating that. "My mother must have had her reasons for putting it the way she did to your dad, the clues to Sarah's identity. And I think the reason was that she knew it was time. In that she was running out of time herself, and because it was time for Sarah to come home. Time for Sarah to be with her own great love. And time for your father to find his. They happened to be one and the same."

Carson closed his eyes. She could feel him internally shaking his head even though he sat ramrod-straight.

"This is what I know about life and how it works, Olivia," he said. "If you're *there*, if you show up, if you do the work—you might get what you want. That's how things happen. Period. Not via a crystal ball." And this time he did bolt up. He ran a hand through his thick, dark hair and let out a breath. "I need to get home to my son."

She didn't know how to argue with what he was saying. There was no argument. He was right. But he was ignoring the whole other side of the coin. Hope, faith, love—need. All things you couldn't see or touch. You *felt* those things.

She walked Carson to the door and opened it. She half expected him to rush out without saying goodbye, but he stopped in the doorway and turned. He reached up his hand and touched her face, and then gave her something of a nod before walking to his car.

Unsettled, her heart heavy, Olivia shut the door and sat back down on the couch. She pulled Sweetie up onto her lap and held her close and knew with total crystal-ball clarity that she'd fallen in love with Carson Ford. She picked up Sweetie and walked past the red velvet curtains into the fortune-telling nook. The real crystal ball in its holder sat on the table. She leaned over to look inside it but saw nothing, just her reflection and Sweetie's face. "Is Carson the one for me or am I headed for heartbreak?" she asked.

She didn't expect an answer and didn't get one.

Until Sweetie let out one meow and nuzzled her cheek.

"Is that a yes or a no?" she asked the cat.

Sweetie nuzzled again. Olivia liked to think that was cat for *yes*. But a moment later, Olivia was back to "unclear at this time" like from the old Magic 8 Ball she and her friends used to play with at sleepovers.

She wasn't so sure she would ask again later, though. Maybe sometimes it was better not to know a thing about what would happen.

Chapter Ten

Carson spent the next morning with his son. After making Danny his favorite chocolate-chip-and-banana pancakes for breakfast, they went to the playground, then the library for story hour, then home for a nap. When Danny woke up, they played hide-and-seek in the backyard and a little T-ball, then headed in to await the sitter. Carson didn't want to leave the little guy. He gave Danny a big hug, very aware that he was about to pick up Joey Johnson for the trip over to confront his father.

I'll always be here for you, Carson thought, giving Danny a kiss on the head before heading out.

He'd needed today. Much of it spent with Danny and now on his work. Some time away from Olivia and fortune-telling seemed the ticket, until he realized all he was doing was thinking about her. At the playground, he heard a caregiver singing a song to a toddler falling asleep in her arms, and he'd found himself wishing Olivia could be there with them. And when he'd pushed Danny on the toddler swings, he felt strangely bereft, like something was missing. Someone. Olivia. He wanted her beside him, singing that meatball song and wearing that skirt with the bulldogs on it.

What he really needed was a bracing cup of coffee and to focus on his work, which this afternoon meant taking Joey to the rodeo barns. He had no idea what to expect, how this was going to play out, and he'd made sure to call Joey's mom last night to make sure she knew it might not go well and that Joey needed to be braced for that.

When he arrived at the Johnsons', Joey was waiting for him on the steps. Carson waved at his mom, who was standing at the window, and off they went. Joey was silent in the car on the way there, holding a letter in his hand from his mom to his father. Joey had explained the letter said that his mother wanted nothing from Steve Johnson except for him to open his life to let Joey in, that she would drive him out to visit once a week or more, depending on what they were both comfortable with.

As Carson pulled into a spot at the rodeo grounds, Joey fell apart. The boy's shoulders began quaking and he just sat there crying, holding his letter.

Carson turned off the ignition and turned to face Joey. "Hey. You know what the most important thing about today is? No matter what happens? That you're here. That you tried. No matter what happens, Joey, you'll always know that. Trying is everything."

"But what if he doesn't even recognize me?" Joey

asks. "Or what if he does and he just walks away?" Tears fell down the boy's freckled cheeks.

His heart clenching, Carson repeated, "You'll know you tried. That's all you can do sometimes. But that way you'll have no regrets because you did what you could. You're a great kid, Joey."

Joey wiped under his eyes and took a deep breath. "Is it time?" he asked, looking up at Carson, then at the dashboard clock. His father got off work in a few minutes.

"It's just about time," Carson said. "Let's go."

Every figurative finger crossed, he walked Joey out to the barns. Two men came out first, their Stetsons pulled down low against the bright sunshine, and he could feel Joey practically jump beside him. Neither man was his father, though. Then another cowboy, and a cowgirl carrying a saddle.

Finally, a couple minutes later, as he and Joey were just steps from the barn, another man came out. Steve Johnson. He was carrying a knapsack over his shoulder and wearing a black cowboy hat.

Joey stopped in his tracks. "Dad?" he said, almost in a whisper.

Steve glanced over their way and froze. "Joey? My God, Joey?"

Joey nodded and the two walked toward each other, Steve throwing down the knapsack and running over to his son.

The cowboy hugged him tight. "I can't believe it's really you."

"It's me," Joey said.

Carson explained who he was and that Joey had hired him to track him down solely so that the two could have a father-and-son relationship, that this wasn't about anything else. Joey handed over the letter, and at the obviously familiar handwriting, Steve froze, then opened it and read it. He put in his pocket.

"I'm sorry for just leaving you," Steve said, looking down at the ground. "I didn't mean to stay away. I just had some problems I had to take care of. And then one day became a week and then a month and then a year, then more. And I never felt like I could come back."

"Why?" Joey asked. Carson could tell from the boy's expression that it was the question he wanted answered more than anything else.

"I guess because I'd been gone so long and thought you hated me. You'd have every right."

"I don't hate you," Joey said, his voice breaking. "I miss you."

"I've missed you like crazy," Steve said, pulling him into another hug.

Carson directed the two to a picnic table by the barns to talk privately. A half hour later, they came over to where Carson waited. Steve said he was going to call Joey's mom and make arrangements to pick up Joey every Saturday. Carson was so damned happy for Joey he almost did a fist pump. Sometimes, things really worked out. Carson liked those times.

He extended his hand and Steve shook it. "I'm very glad to hear it."

The entire way back home, Joey talked nonstop about the things his dad had told him, how he'd learned how to be a cowboy and had even won a few bronc-riding competitions. He'd asked a ton of questions about Joey, how he liked school and what he was learning and what he liked to do after school.

"Wow, can you imagine if I didn't hire you to find him?" Joey asked, his manner, his voice, his whole bearing completely different than on the way over. "He'd still be gone and I'd still be always wondering about my dad. Now he's coming to pick me up on Saturday for a whole day together."

"You were incredibly brave," Carson said. "I've got to hand it to you. And I'm very happy with how things turned out."

Joey Johnson was exceptionally brave. Carson thought about all the times he'd wanted to confront his dad, who'd been physically there, sometimes, anyway, about always canceling their plans or not turning up to birthday celebrations or traveling on holidays for business, but he'd always felt too proud to let anyone know how disappointed and hurt he'd been. So he'd kept it all bottled up inside, giving himself stomachaches. His mother had known; she'd been able to tell by his expression, but Carson had never opened up to her much about it.

But here, a nine-year-old had gone all out, risking everything to *try*. The afternoon could have gone very differently, very painfully. As a PI, Carson had experienced quite a few of those reunions. There were some people, like his old neighbor's son, who really didn't want to be found.

But some people, people who drove right into Blue Gulch, clearly did. And so it was time to find Sarah Mack once and for all and he would if he had to drive down every road of every street in the county and surrounding ones. He'd find that little yellow car; he'd find Sarah, and he'd give Olivia what she needed: her aunt.

As he turned onto the road toward Oak Creek, he

realized something. He suddenly wanted to find Sarah
Mack more for Olivia's sake than to prove to his father
that the woman wasn't his second great love, that he'd
feel the same nothing at the sight of her as he had for
the stylist in the Oak Creek salon.

Which meant he'd come to care about Olivia Mack
way too much.

And that a nine-year-old kid was a hell of a lot
braver than he was.

Carson dropped off Joey and talked with his relieved
mom a bit, then hit the road, starting with the main
street of Oak Creek to look for the yellow Beetle. For
all they know, Sarah Mack lived in Oak Creek, just a
town away from Blue Gulch. But he didn't see the car
and driving through town got him nowhere, too. He
was going to try the town to the east, then decided he'd
try Blue Gulch again. If Sarah had gone there once—
who knew how many times she'd driven around Blue
Gulch, really—she would go back. He had no doubt
that the woman had driven through town to catch a
glimpse of her niece.

The car wasn't on Blue Gulch Street or in any of the
parking spots or lots. But when he turned onto a side
road and pulled into the parking lot behind the library,
there it was, way in the back, the last spot, between the
brick wall of a building and a minivan. He checked the
plate to make sure—it was definitely Sarah Mack's car.

Yes! Thank you, universe.

Adrenaline coursing through him, Carson parked
and headed inside the library, which wasn't very
crowded, but there was no sign of a woman match-
ing Sarah's description. He did another sweep, just in

case he'd missed her. As politely as possible he excused himself from the children's librarian who'd come over to say hello and ask how Danny was. Normally, he'd love to talk about his favorite subject—his son—but he had an aunt to find.

He headed out through the front door of the library and looked around, trying to spot a tall, forty-eight-year-old woman with long auburn hair, probably curly, per Olivia. Blue Gulch Street was crowded today with people walking around for day two of the sidewalk sale, so spotting anyone wasn't easy. His dad's closest neighbors were heading into the Blue Gulch coffee shop with lots of shopping bags in their hands. And there were the Hurleys—Essie Hurley, owner of Hurley's Homestyle Kitchen and the food truck that Olivia worked in, and her three granddaughters with their husbands. Annabel and West, with a baby in a carrier on his chest, and their little girl. Georgia and Nick—the detective who'd called him about Sarah Mack's car in the first place—with a baby in a stroller. And Clementine and Logan with a pair of cute young twins and a girl around nine or ten. The big family, whom Carson had met at Nick's wedding, was setting down blankets on the town green, picnic baskets as corner weights. A few yards away, one of Danny's day care mates and his family were trying to teach a puppy to sit. He scanned the crowded green, looking for anyone who fit the bill.

Wait a minute. Could that be her?

Sitting across the square, on one of the small boulders that dotted the far edges of the town green and doubled as low seats, was a woman who looked to be in her midforties, tall, wearing huge black sunglasses and a gray cap. An auburn ponytail lay on one shoulder. She was alone and seemed to be people watching, but she was sitting across from the food truck just on the other side of the square. Because she was trying to catch a glimpse of her niece? She wore a casual gray dress—maybe so she wouldn't stand out.

He had a pretty good feeling the woman was Sarah Mack. He pulled out his phone and pressed in Olivia's telephone number, his heart beating ten miles a minute.

Olivia hurried out of her house, Carson's phone call just a moment ago echoing in her mind. He was ninety-nine percent sure that her aunt was sitting on the town green, looking toward the Hurley's food truck. Olivia lived just a couple minutes away by foot. *Please don't be gone when I get there*, she thought.

At the corner of Blue Gulch Street, she saw Carson standing in front of the coffee shop, sipping from a take-out cup. He nodded across the green and she followed the direction of his gaze.

Every molecule in her body seemed to speed up and slow down at the same time. The woman sitting there in the huge sunglasses was Aunt Sarah. She'd know her anywhere, big black lenses covering her face or not.

As she walked toward her aunt from the right, away from where Sarah was looking, she could see the silver glint of the tattoo on her ankle. The brush. As she drew closer, she could see the hot pink blow-dryer. Aunt Sarah. She was really here.

She walked closer, unsure if she could call out or just present herself.

Finally, she was just steps away.

"Aunt Sarah," she said softly.

Sarah started and turned and whipped off her sunglasses. "Olivia. Olivia!" She rushed over and enveloped Olivia into a hug.

"I can't believe you just found me," Sarah said, her green eyes glistening with tears. "I've been hanging around town the past few days, looking for glimpses of you. I wasn't ready to just knock on your door. I heard in town from bits here and there that you run the food truck, so I thought I'd catch a glimpse of you working."

"Why have you come now?" Olivia asked. "I mean, was there a specific reason you chose now?"

"I can't explain it," Sarah said. "I just had this overpowering urge the last few weeks to see you, even from a distance."

"Mom died," Olivia said on a whisper, barely able to say the words.

Sarah's expression clouded over. "I know. I…felt it, I guess. And because of that, I looked for the obituary until there it was. I did attend the funeral in disguise. I just wasn't ready to see you."

"But why?" Olivia asked. "I don't understand. I've never understood."

Sarah took a deep breath. "Let's talk about this in private."

While her aunt sat on the sofa in the living room of Olivia's house, making baby talk to Sweetie about how much she missed the dear old cat, Olivia put together a cheese-and-cracker plate in the kitchen, thinking that Sarah and Edmund already had the warm-hearted baby talk in common. She smiled, imagining the two meeting for the first time, thunderstruck at the sight of each other.

But there was a lot to get through before she'd even

raise the subject of Miranda's prediction. Such as what
had kept her aunt away for so long. She poured two
glasses of white wine and set everything on a tray, her
hands trembling a bit with anticipation of finally learning what had come between the sisters.

As she was bringing the tray into the living room,
she half expected to find her aunt gone. But there she
sat, her beautiful green eyes giving nothing away, her
curly auburn hair in a long ponytail off to one side.
Again, Olivia's gaze locked on the little tattoo on her
ankle. Her aunt, now forty-eight, hadn't changed a whit
in five years.

She handed Sarah a glass of wine, and they clinked.
She'd hoped her aunt might make a toast—to their re-
union, to the future—but she didn't. Perhaps Sarah felt
toasts might be better saved until everything was said.

"Will you tell me why you left five years ago?" Olivia
asked as she sat down across from Sarah.

Sarah took a deep breath and let it out. She sipped
her wine, put it down and crossed her arms over her
chest, as if protecting herself from what she was about
to say. "A very long time ago, when I was just sixteen
years old, I discovered I was pregnant. The father, my
then boyfriend, immediately broke up with me and insisted it couldn't be his. My mother, very firmly, told
me that for the sake of the babies, I had to give them
up for adoption and that there would be no discussion."

"Babies?" Olivia whispered. Not baby. *Babies*.

She nodded. "Yes, babies. My mother knew before
I did that I was pregnant with twins. She sent me away
to a home for pregnant teenagers in Houston. I never
held the babies or saw them. But I did hear one of the
nurses say that they were boys. Fraternal twins."

"I had no idea," Olivia said, thinking of Sarah at only sixteen, pregnant, sent away. How scary it must have been.

"I came back home and never talked about it," Sarah continued. "My mother refused to discuss it, never brought it up, not once, and my sister was only fourteen. Miranda asked questions, but I always cut her off and eventually she stopped. I just turned inward and tried to pretend the whole thing had been a dream."

"Oh, Aunt Sarah. It must have been so hard. You were so young."

She sipped her wine and looked away as if trying to stop a memory. "When I was seventeen and my gift was supposed to make itself known, it didn't. I thought I was being blamed for getting pregnant, for giving away the twins. I shut down even more." Sarah stood up and walked over to the windows, looking out at the backyard.

"Did your gift ever materialize?" Olivia asked.

Sarah turned to face her. "No. I don't know why. My mother said that sometimes it skipped a generation or a person, that her aunt didn't have a gift. But when Miranda turned seventeen and it became clear she had the gift of predicting the future, I felt so jealous. I kept my distance from her and told her she was never, ever, to tell me anything about my future or I'd never speak to her again. So she never did."

"Until five years ago?" Olivia asked, her heart in her throat.

Sarah nodded. "Until five years ago. Miranda told me that she knew, just knew, that one of the twins—who'd been adopted separately—was desperately trying to find me and having no luck. I told her to stop, that I didn't want to hear it. I reminded her that she promised me she'd never tell me anything about my future, and she said it wasn't *my* future—it was the boys'. I was so upset with her. This was my business, not hers."

"But she didn't stop?" Olivia asked. Her mother could be relentless when she felt strongly about something. She must have felt *very* strongly about what she was telling her sister.

"Miranda kept telling me to just check with the adoption agency, that I'd find contact information there, that she *knew* it was important I do so. I told her to mind her own business, that I didn't want to hear more, that I couldn't handle it. She said I *had* to handle it. That night, I packed my things and left."

"Oh, Aunt Sarah, it must be hard for you to even talk about. I'm so sorry."

Her aunt's face crumped for a moment. "It's very hard. For so long I didn't let myself even think about being pregnant or all my hopes and dreams that somehow, I could just run away and have the twins. But I was so afraid. I had no one. I was just sixteen. My mother was so firm about how things would be. The night I gave birth, when it was all over, I literally felt something inside my chest shutter closed."

Olivia rushed over to her aunt and wrapped her arms around her. Sarah stiffened, but finally she embraced Olivia and allowed the hug, the comfort.

"Until five years ago, I never allowed myself to think about that night. The loss. The heartbreak. I'm so sorry I left you behind, Livvy. I was so unfair to you. When I knew that Miranda passed away, I began feeling terrible shame and guilt that I hadn't listened to her, that I let my own fear keep me from helping the boys—or one of them. But I was so shut down about it."

Olivia could well imagine how scared and alone her aunt had felt—thirty-two years ago and five years ago. And now, as well. "I understand, Aunt Sarah. I really do."

"And lately," Sarah continued, "these past few weeks, I can't explain it, but I feel ready to check that registry and see if they...or one, anyway, is looking for me. I've been worried that maybe Miranda's insistence was because she knew one or both needed a blood relative for something health-related." She shook her head, tears glistening in her eyes. "What if I'm too late?"

"Aunt Sarah, maybe she just thought it was time for you to make peace with your past. Perhaps she foresaw that the twins simply wanted to find their birth mother, which is natural."

"Perhaps."

Olivia waited for Sarah to continue, but her aunt remained silent and turned back to the window again.

Olivia sensed that her aunt needed a break from the conversation. "Where do you live?" she asked.

Sarah turned around. "In Tuckerville. I'm still a hairstylist. When I first moved there, I made up a phony last name and worked off the books in a busy salon, and when I built up a following in a few months, I began working out of my home. I have an over-the-top stage name that I go by professionally—Starlight Smith. I was trying to make myself difficult to find—by anyone." She turned away again and her shoulders started shaking.

Olivia wrapped her arms around her aunt, who began sobbing. "I'm so glad you told me. And that you're here. No matter what, Sarah, we're family and we belong together."

Sarah squeezed her hand. "I think I need to rest. Is the guest room still a guest room?"

Olivia nodded. "Yup."

As Sarah headed down the hall, she turned and said, "I promise I won't flee. I do feel a little shaky about talking about the twins. They're thirty-two years old now. Grown men who very likely have families of their own." She closed her eyes. "I'd better go lie down for a bit."

She disappeared into the guest room with Sweetie following.

Olivia sank down on the sofa, starting to process everything she'd learned. If her aunt really did want to track down the twins, Carson could help.

What she would give to unload to him right now, feel his strong arms around her.

"Olivia?" Sarah called.

Olivia went into the guest room. "Do you need something?"

"Your mom knew I loved her, right?" Sarah asked, tears glistening again. "I just need to know that she did."

Olivia sat on the edge of the bed. "She did know. She told me that constantly. When you first left, I kept pestering her to tell me what happened, that I'd heard the tail end of an argument. And she'd always say, 'We did have an argument and Sarah needs to process it in her own way on her own time. She loves us, even though she left. Always remember that.'"

Sarah reached over and squeezed Olivia's hand. "I

knew she'd understand. Even if she didn't agree. I feel a lot better about that."

"While she was dying, she asked me to promise to find you so that I could deliver a letter and a family heirloom. I assured her I would. Would you like the letter and heirloom now?"

"Okay," she said.

Olivia rushed to her bedroom and retrieved the letter and the box with the gold bangle bracelet that had both sisters' names engraved on it. It had been their grandmother's.

The letter was sealed with red wax but it wasn't very long since the envelope was so thin. Olivia had always wondered what it said, but she wouldn't ask unless Sarah wanted to share it.

She left her aunt alone to read the letter. Ten minutes later, Sarah came into the kitchen, where Olivia was tidying up.

"Do you want to read the letter?" Sarah asked, handing it over. Olivia almost gasped when she realized her aunt was wearing the gold bangle. The letter must have done its job.

Olivia nodded and took it. The letter was handwritten on thin white stationery in black ink.

Dear Sarah,

I'm sorry that I drove you away. It's always been a fine line for me to know when to stay silent. I should have respected your feelings. I hope you'll forgive me. If you do, I'll know it.

All my love,

Your sister, Miranda

"I do forgive her," Sarah said, brushing tears from under her eyes. "And you know, I do think she knows it," she added, looking toward the ceiling.

Olivia hugged her aunt, then put the letter back in the envelope.

"I was thinking about hiring a private investigator to help me find the twins," Sarah said. "If they have been looking for me, I want them to be able to contact me. And if they haven't been looking, well, I'll just leave my contact information so that they can find me if they ever decide to do so. I suppose I could start with the adoption agency and the registry, but I think I would rather have someone I trust go through the steps and arrange things for me."

Olivia smiled. "I know just the guy."

Chapter Eleven

Over dinner, Olivia explained the whole story to her aunt, about Carson barging up to the food truck, the prediction about his father's second great love being a green-eyed hairstylist named Sarah with a small tattoo of a brush and a blow-dryer on her ankle and the road trips to find her.

The more she talked, the more Olivia became aware of her aunt's stricken expression.

"I want no part of this," Sarah said through gritted teeth. She stood up and grabbed her tote bag and then rushed out the door.

Oh, no. No, no, no.

"Sarah, wait!" Olivia called, rushing after her. She saw her aunt hurrying toward the town green.

Olivia stepped back inside and closed her eyes. Why hasn't she anticipated that her aunt wouldn't want any part of her mother's fortune-telling or prediction? Aunt Sarah was clearly uncomfortable with all that. Especially because Miranda had "seen" something regarding the twins, or one of them, anyway, and it had driven Sarah away. Olivia should have known Sarah would react negatively to being a part of Miranda's prediction.

Head against the wall, she thought, very tempted to thunk her forehead against the front door. She should have handled this better. But she'd simply told the truth. She couldn't *not* tell Sarah about the prediction, particularly since the one private investigator Olivia knew— and trusted with all her heart—was the son of Sarah's predicted great love. Ugh. Why would Sarah be comfortable with that? Of course she wouldn't be.

What a mess. Just like it was in the beginning, when Carson *had* barged up to the food truck, full of preconceived notions.

She grabbed her phone and called Sarah, thanking her lucky stars that her aunt had given Olivia her cell phone number and address while they were cooking together. She pressed in the number. Voice mail.

"Sarah, I'm sorry I was so insensitive," Olivia said. "I know you don't like any of this. Please don't leave again. Can we please just talk?"

She put the phone away, unsure what to do. Edmund Ford came to mind—that wonderful, kind, doting grandfather. Meeting his Sarah meant everything to Edmund. What if Sarah came back and said there was no way she was meeting some man her sister thought was her great love? She had every right not to, but now Olivia felt for Edmund Ford.

She pulled out her phone again and called Carson. She wouldn't betray her aunt's confidence about the twins, certainly not concerning such a personal subject, but she needed to hear his voice, get his perspective. He'd found Sarah for her. Maybe he could find her again.

He answered immediately. "Let me try talking to her," Carson said. "I don't know what the big argument between the sisters was about, but I do know how *I* feel about the prediction and my dad. Once she hears what I have to say about the whole thing, she may agree to meet my dad just so I can be proven right and we can all get on with our lives, and you and Sarah can rebuild your relationship."

We can all get on with our lives... Her heart clenched as she gave Carson Sarah's address and telephone number.

"Would you mind watching Danny while I go to her house?" he asked.

"Of course," she said. "I'll come right over." She paused, realizing she had to tell him something, something he might not like hearing. "Carson, if Sarah will talk to you and she agrees to meet your dad, you do need to accept that it's going to be love at first sight. My mother's predictions were rarely wrong."

"I'm hardly worried about that, Olivia. Power of suggestion. People make things so. You can make yourself believe what you want. My dad might be affected by the prediction and all starry-eyed and full of hope, but clearly your aunt wants no part of it. She won't be walking into the situation expecting to be blown away by love."

My aunt knows that her sister's gift was very real, though, Olivia wanted to counter. From the time Miranda was seventeen until five years ago, Sarah had witnessed her predictions come true constantly. But Olivia knew to let it go for now. "We'll see," she said gently.

"Yes, we will."

If he could convince Sarah to meet Edmund in the first place. Olivia wasn't so sure about that.

"I can't believe she's gone again," Olivia said when Carson opened the door of his house and let her in. "I just got her back."

He squeezed her hand, his heart going out to her. "Let me see what I can do." He looked over at Danny, who was sitting in his playpen, squeezing his new stuffed panda that sang a silly song. "Danny, look who's here to play with you while I go do some work."

Danny stood up. "Liva!"

Carson loved watching Olivia's expression go from worried to pure happiness at the sight of the toddler holding out his arms for her to scoop him up.

She hurried over to Danny and picked him up, giving him a cuddle. "I'm so happy to see you, Danny. Want to do a puzzle?" she asked, pointing at the four-piece puzzle of a dolphin.

"See you two later," Carson said, kissing the top of Danny's head. "Everything will be okay."

"I didn't think you believed in that kind of thing," she said with a bit of a sad smile.

He narrowed his eyes at her. He wasn't going to say that it was just something people said because he didn't go around making platitudes about important things. He really did think this would work out okay. He'd state the facts to her aunt, who seemed levelheaded, and she'd agree to meet his dad to get it out of the way and off the table. Sarah and Edmund would feel absolutely nothing for each other, and that would be that.

"Instinct. Gut reaction. Those have validity," he said.

"Thanks for doing this." With Danny in her arms, she smiled at the little boy, who was twirling a long lock of her silky brown hair.

His own smile faltered. He was doing this so that he could put an end to it. But at least he'd bring Olivia and Sarah back together again. That was what this was all about.

For the past twenty minutes, Danny had sat in Olivia's lap on the overstuffed rocker by the window as she read him the same picture book four times, pointing at the pages and giggling. A talking monkey who liked hamburgers was very funny stuff to a toddler.

As she closed the book, grateful that Danny didn't ask her to read it a fifth time, she wondered what was going on with Carson and her aunt right now. Had Carson gotten ahold of Sarah? Had she refused to talk to him? Carson could be pretty persuasive. Hadn't he gotten her to agree to come to his father's house that first day he stormed up to the food truck?

"Monkey?" Danny asked, scrambling off her lap and looking around his toy area in the family room. "Monkey?" he said, picking up stuffed animals and tossing them aside. "Monkey?"

"I'll help you look," she said, getting up from the rocking chair.

She missed the feel of Danny against her. She loved the way his hair smelled, like baby shampoo. She loved the little weight of him. She loved the way the expression in his big hazel-green eyes changed every other second with worry or delight as the monkey in the book gobbled up every hamburger in town and got a belly-ache. She loved *him*.

So what was going to happen now? What was Olivia supposed to do with all this…love? Carson didn't seem to want it. Danny wasn't hers to give it to. And if Carson had his way, the three Fords would be out of her life in a matter of time, once he got his father and Sarah to-gether to prove—supposedly—that there was no spark, no connection. No great love happening.

Her cell phone rang and Olivia grabbed it out of her pocket, keeping an eye on Danny as she kept looking for the stuffed monkey. It was Dory.

"Guess what!" Dory practically screamed in her ear. "I did it! I got the loan. I'm going to save the bakery on my own."

Olivia's heart leaped for her friend. "I'm so happy for you! Let me know when you're free to celebrate with one of your amazing cupcakes, on me, of course."

"Thanks," Dory said. "And thanks for being there and listening. I had a long talk with Beaufort about everything—and I mean everything. Do you know that his mother threatened to sue me for public humiliation and the cost of the engagement toast gathering? Beau-fort managed to calm her down."

Olivia could just picture Annalee Harrington with steam coming out of her ears. "His mother must be scrambling to undo all the publicity she generated."

"Well, it's the strangest thing, Olivia. When I told Beaufort about the loan—of course, I didn't use his bank, Texas Trust—he was truly happy for me. He said our whole romance might have been put on the fast track by his ambition-crazed family, but that he has real feelings for me. He asked if we could get together to talk, maybe start over from scratch and see if there is something real underneath everything—no photographers or reporters or mothers. I reminded him that I planned to work every day in my bakery, that it's as important to me as running for mayor is for him, and he finally got it."

Olivia smiled. "Do you think there's a chance for you two?"

"I honestly don't know. I do like Beaufort an awful lot. But I'm not in love—as your mother made me focus on. All this time I thought she was saying that he wasn't the one for me. But she was just telling me to look into my heart, to acknowledge my feelings or lack thereof. I started things with Beaufort for the same reason he started things with me—because we could each help each other out. Now, we want to see what's there with no eye at the future. Just each other."

"That's great, Dory. I'm doubly happy for you."

As Dory said goodbye and Olivia pocketed the phone, she realized her friend was right; her mother had never said Beaufort wasn't "the one" for Dory. He could be. But before, Dory wasn't listening to her heart, which had been telling her to fix her life herself and not exchange herself and that heart so that someone else could make things all better.

Her mother was a smart cookie. Insightful. She just *knew.* Based on what Miranda had told Dory and her refusal to say anything else, Olivia had the feeling that Beaufort Harrington might well be the one for Dory and that Madam Miranda had put Dory on the path to questioning what she was doing. Now Dory had rescued herself—and might still get the handsome knight.

If only I knew what would happen in my own life, she thought, again wondering if Carson was talking to Sarah that very moment.

"Monkey!" Danny said, pointing down the hall. He took off running.

She followed, pausing as Danny raced into his father's bedroom. Olivia didn't think she should be going into Carson's room, but she couldn't exactly let Danny run around unattended. She stood in the doorway as he looked around the large room for the stuffed monkey.

A king-size bed was against the back wall, centered between two end tables, a short stack of books on one. As Danny climbed onto the bed, she saw that a pile of stuffed animals was wedged between the pillows. Including a yellow monkey. In the corner of the room by the windows was a little play area with a foam interlocking mat decorated with letters and numbers. Building blocks, toys, more stuffed animals. This wasn't exactly Carson's bachelor lair or sanctuary. He was a dad through and through.

Danny flopped backward on the bed, holding up the yellow monkey and making him dance. Olivia sat down next to him, sinking into the plushness of the navy-and-white comforter. She couldn't help imagining Carson coming out of the master bathroom, naked, damp, his dark hair slicked back.

She allowed herself to push away all that was on her mind and just think of Carson kissing her.

Until a yellow sock monkey started dancing on her thigh. "Hi, Liva! Monkey!"

She blinked away thoughts of a naked Carson to focus on the here and now.

"Catch?" Danny asked, scrambling off the bed so slowly that she could have caught him in two seconds. He went giggling out of the room.

"I'm gonna get you!" she said, chasing him in slow motion.

You've already caught me, she thought. *And so has your dad.*

It was a hell of a lot easier to find Sarah Mack when number one, Carson knew her address, and number two, she was sitting on the steps of her house, a small yellow bungalow that reminded him of Olivia's. His relief at seeing her there didn't go unnoticed by him. He wanted to make Olivia happy.

As he approached, Sarah was looking away, a worried look in her eyes.

"Sarah? I'm Carson Ford, Olivia's...friend. I'm the son of the man who's supposed to be your great love."

She turned toward him, squinting a bit at the setting sun. "The private investigator?"

He nodded. "I'm sure Olivia told you that I don't want any part in this prediction business, either. To me, it's nonsense and make-believe and the power of suggestion. The only reason I barged into Olivia's life was to ask her to tell my father that her mother was a scam artist."

"She wasn't, though, Carson. My sister was the real deal. That's why I estranged myself from her and her daughter. Did Olivia tell you about that?"

He shook his head. "I only know that you and your sister had an argument and you left five years ago."

"My sister had the gift of knowing. She would get a feeling and simply know. When she told me, five years ago, that one of the twin boys I gave up for adoption at age sixteen was looking for me, that it was important that I contact him, I—I just couldn't handle it. I shut down that part of myself for so long."

"I can understand that," he said, sitting down beside her, keeping enough distance between them. He made sure to give her space, to not bombard her with questions, to let her talk at her own pace.

"I'm not interested in the prediction my sister made to your father, Carson. I don't want any part of that. It's taken me this long—five years—to finally accept what my sister told me about the twins. I'm ready to start the process to find them. I wasn't ready then."

"If you're ready, I can help you," he said. "It would be my pleasure."

She glanced at him, suspicion in her eyes. "Because you want me to meet your dad, right?"

"I would help you regardless, Sarah. But yes, I do want you to meet my father only to put an end to this fortune nonsense. You say your sister had a gift, Olivia says she had a gift. There are supposedly hundreds, thousands of people who believed she had a gift. Well, I don't believe in any of that mumbo jumbo. I believe in reality and facts and, yeah, I rely heavily on my instincts, but that's not seeing into the future. That's about trusting yourself."

"Carson, I'm not sure it's a good idea that I meet your father. I'm sorry, but I would prefer not to."

He got it, he really did. He wished he didn't have to push it; the woman had enough on her mind. For one, she'd just reunited with her niece. Now she'd be undertaking something that would be very emotional for her, push all kinds of buttons: finding the twins she gave up for adoption decades ago. But his father was counting on him. If Carson could just get the love prediction off the table, everyone could focus on their lives again.

"I just need five minutes of your time, Sarah. That's it. Five minutes for you and my dad to take one look each other and feel absolutely nothing. Yeah, he'll be disappointed since he's put so much stock in this green-eyed hairstylist named Sarah being his second great love, but when he sees it's meaningless, that he feels nothing, he'll be free to pursue love with someone *he* chooses, someone he falls for naturally."

Yes, he thought. That was really the point here. He wanted his dad to be happy and find love—his second great love. He truly did. And Edmund would find it once he realized there was nothing between him and Sarah Mack.

"Carson, I really don't want to be put in the position of having to disappoint your father. That seems unfair. So why not just leave it alone? I've got so much on my mind about the possibility of meeting the twins that love and romance are the last things I want."

It finally dawned on Carson that Sarah was saying that she knew his father would fall instantly in love. Because Madam Miranda had said they were destined for each other.

Oh, come on. Was everyone crazy but him?

"My father meets a lot of women in the course of a day," Carson said. "He will meet you and feel the way he does about the vice president of sales or the barista at the coffee shop or the children's librarian who helps him pick books for my son. Please, Sarah. It's all he can think about lately—the mystery woman he's meant to be with. Just let him see it's not meant to be and that will be that."

"It's not meant to be—*for me*," she said. "I guess I can help on that end, since I have no intention of getting involved with any man right now."

Finally. "So you'll meet him? Perhaps you can come for dinner tomorrow night at my house? Neutral turf. Six thirty?"

"And you'll help me find the twins?" she asked.

He nodded and they both stood up.

"Carson, the family gift seems to have skipped me. But my sister *did* have the ability to see beyond. That is just the truth. Not mumbo jumbo or nonsense. The truth."

He stared at her. "Right. So when you meet my father, there'll be fireworks exploding overhead and parades marching and instant love?"

Sarah raised an eyebrow. "I'm just saying that since my sister predicted that I'm the one for your dad, he will very likely feel those fireworks and hear that parade when he meets me."

He won't, Carson thought. *Not a single boom or clang of the cymbals. And come on, she's so sure my dad will fall for her, but she doesn't seem worried one bit about resisting him.* "So it doesn't work both ways? You can be the one for him, but he may not be the one for you?"

"Oh, it works both ways," she said. "But that doesn't mean I have to give in to it. I'm a very strong-willed person, Carson. Clearly. And as I've said, I'm not interested in love. I just want to reconnect with the twins I gave up, have some peace by knowing that they're all right, and then I'll move on. I'd like to keep up my relationship with Olivia, though. I feel terrible that I estranged myself from her. And I should have been there for her these past two months since she lost her mother."

"Well, you're here now." He pictured Olivia, playing with Danny, singing to him, hoping that Carson was able to convince her aunt to come back. He didn't want Olivia hurt. He wanted to be happy. He gave her his address. "Six thirty, tomorrow night."

"I'll be there. But I'm not sure you're going to get what you want. You may end up with a bigger problem."

"Meaning?" Carson drew in a deep breath.

Sarah Mack stood up and lifted her chin. "Might as well wait till you cross that bridge, as they say."

He didn't want to cross whatever bridge she was referring to.

Chapter Twelve

"Dad?" Carson called out as he let himself in his father's house in Blue Gulch the next morning.

He had no idea how this was going to turn out—tonight, dinner at his house. With his father. Sarah. And Olivia, of course.

"In the kitchen," his dad called back.

Carson entered the kitchen to find his dad trying to frost a very lopsided cake. Except every time Edmund swiped the rubber spatula against the side of the vanilla sponge, the frosting took off a slab of the cake.

"Yesterday I promised Danny I'd bake him a cake for his half birthday," Edmund said, frosting all over the striped apron he wore and a glob on his shearling house slipper. "It might not *look* good, but it'll *taste* good. That's what counts."

Carson froze, staring from the cake to his father.

What would he do without this man? What would Danny do without him? "You're a great grandfather," he said, looking at the ridiculous cake again. Carson wouldn't be surprised if it caved in on itself. "Danny is very, very lucky to have you."

Edmund lifted his chin, the way he did when he was touched by praise. "Maybe I'm trying to make up for what I didn't do the first time around. When I had a terrific eighteen-month-old of my own running around my house in Oak Creek and I was too busy with my work and committees and the town council. I let you down and I let your mother down." He dropped the rubber spatula on the counter, another glob of chocolate icing splattering against his apron. "I won't let Danny down."

"Dad, you know what I've been realizing? When I was a kid, you did what felt right to you. You worked. Hard. The way you saw it, you were supporting your family and so you put work ahead of everything so that nothing would interfere. I never understood that before."

"That doesn't make it right. I wasn't there for you, Carson. And I wasn't there for your mother." He took a deep breath. "I've been doing a lot of thinking the past couple of days. I'm calling off the hunt for Sarah. After the way I lived my life when I had everything a man could want, I have no business trying to find a second great love. I had my chance the first time around and I blew it. Right now, I'm going to focus on Danny. He only has one parent. I'm going to make up for everything he doesn't have."

Carson's stomach twisted. "Dad, you *do* have a right to a second chance and a second love. You're a completely different person than you were when I was growing up. You're here, one hundred percent for both me and Danny. When Jodie left and I realized she wasn't coming back, *you* were there in the NICU. You were there when I was scared to death that my newborn son might not make it. And you've been by my side ever since, for eighteen months. You've been more than an amazing grandfather. You've been an amazing *dad*."

Edmund grabbed him in a bear hug. "You have no idea how much that means to me. How much *you* mean to me. I know you know how much I love Danny. But I also love you with all my heart, Carson. I always have since the day you were born. I'm just better at making it clear these days."

Carson could feel decades' worth of old resentments ungluing from the cells of his body.

Suddenly, Carson wanted his father to take one look at Sarah Mack and hear those parade cymbals clanking and drumbeats, and for fireworks to go off over his head. He wanted cartoon hearts pouring out of his chest as he staggered around, shot by Cupid's arrow. He wanted his father to feel what Carson felt every time he looked at Olivia.

Oh, God.

What?

He loved Olivia?

He loved Olivia.

But he couldn't love her. He'd shut himself down, off, wasn't letting anyone in. Final answer.

And just because you felt something didn't mean you had to give in to it. Wasn't that what Sarah Mack had said last night? She'd meet his dad, and if she felt anything for him, she'd simply not act on it. She wanted to focus on finding the twins she'd given up for adoption. And on her niece, with whom she'd just gotten reunited. She'd closed herself off to love, like Carson, and would simply *not go there*. It was that easy.

Feeling better about everything, except the part about his dad possibly getting hurt, Carson picked up the spatula. "Want some help frosting this cake?"

His dad would not get hurt. His dad would meet Sarah, feel absolutely nothing, be a little disappointed that the prediction was silly nonsense and find his second great love on his own. He'd meet a lovely woman whom *he* chose. Everything *would* work out just fine.

Edmund smiled. "I sure do. I might be good at being a grandfather, but I'm a terrible baker."

"Dad, the reason I stopped by is to tell you that I found Sarah Mack."

His dad stared at him. "What?"

"I found her, Dad. And she's agreed to come to my house for dinner tonight to meet you. I'll warn you—she's not looking for love." *Just like I'm not.*

"I wasn't necessarily looking for love, either," Edmund said. "But the idea presented itself. It's funny—once it did, I couldn't stop thinking about. A second chance. A fresh shot. A new beginning."

Carson frowned. All things he was refusing to take for himself. "Well, just be forewarned that she's got a lot going on right now and doesn't seem very interested in romance."

"I'm not worried," Edmund said. "Madam Miranda said it was so and it'll be so. You can't ignore destiny."

"Well, you can."

"You can *try* to ignore destiny, Carson. There's a big difference."

Carson swallowed.

* * *

Six thirty came and went. So did six thirty-five. Now, as Olivia glanced at the grandfather clock against the wall of the living room in Carson's house, she realized that Carson and Edmund were doing the same thing.

What if her aunt changed her mind? About everything? What if she'd gone back to her incognito life? Although now, Olivia had Sarah's address and telephone number. Of course, that didn't mean her aunt would answer the door or the phone or ever speak to Olivia again. Last night, after Carson had called Olivia and let her know he'd talked to Sarah and that she'd agreed to come to dinner tonight, Olivia had left her aunt a voice mail message. She'd said only that she'd missed her so much the past five years and couldn't bear to lose her again, and that no matter what, to call when she was ready to talk.

So far, she hadn't heard from Sarah. Not last night, not all day today.

"The suspense is killing me," Edmund said. "I'm going to check on Danny."

Danny had been so tuckered out from a fun afternoon of playing with his grandfather that he'd fallen asleep on the car ride over to Carson's and had been effortlessly transferred to his crib.

As Edmund headed down the hall, Olivia peered out the windows. No little yellow car.

Now it was six forty.

"We have to accept that she might not come," Carson said, sitting down on the leather sofa. "She's skittish, that's for sure."

"I can understand why," Olivia said, too jumpy to

sit. Based on what Carson said, even if her aunt fell instantly in love with Edmund, she was going to fight it to focus on her own mission. And to continue to ignore her sister's ability, something she never made peace with.

There was a knock at the door, and Olivia's eyes widened. Carson leaped up.

"She came," Olivia whispered, relief flooding her.

Carson opened the door, Olivia standing behind him.

And there was Sarah Mack, wearing a navy blue dress, her hair in a low ponytail. She carried a small yellow box from Drummond's Bake Shop. One day, if it ever seemed like the right time, Olivia would tell her aunt all about Dory and her own fortune.

"Thank you for coming," Carson said to Sarah. "It means a lot."

Olivia slipped past Carson and hugged her aunt. "I'm so glad you're here."

Sarah smiled at her. "I still can't get over how good it feels to see you, Olivia. Five years without and suddenly now, twice in two days. I've missed you so much."

"Me, too," Olivia said, a little lump forming in her throat.

Sarah handed Carson the box. "Cookies from my favorite bakery in Blue Gulch." She glanced past Carson, looking around the living room. "Is your father here?"

"He's upstairs, checking on my son," Carson said. "Danny's eighteen months. Sometimes my dad says he's going to check on Danny while he's napping and he ends up just sitting there, staring at him sleeping, marveling at his features. I've caught him doing it and it always makes me choke up a little. When you witness love."

Olivia stared at Carson, dumbstruck by what she'd just heard come out of his mouth. Choking up? Witnessing love?

"He sounds like a nice man," Sarah said, her expression a bit strained.

"I'm not trying to make his case, I promise," Carson said. "I just see him differently now so I guess I'm Team Edmund now."

"Wait," Olivia said. "Make his case? Suddenly you're hoping my aunt *does* fall for your dad?"

He took a breath and let it out. "All I know is that I want my father to be happy. I was missing that piece before. There's no scam involved—I know that now. So all that's left is…feelings."

Sarah glanced at the floor. "Or a lack thereof."

Footsteps sounded from the stairs and then down the hall as Edmund's voice carried into the living room. "Of course, I got caught up watching Danny's little face—"

He stopped speaking as he rounded the corner into the living room archway. He stared at Sarah, who was staring at him.

Olivia looked from her aunt to Edmund and back again as though at a soccer match; Carson stood across from her doing the same. Sarah. Edmund. Sarah. Edmund.

"Dad, this is Sarah Mack. Olivia's aunt," Carson said. "Sarah, my father, Edmund Ford."

Edmund stepped into the room, his gaze never leaving Sarah. He was neither smiling nor frowning. His expression was completely neutral, as was Sarah's.

Huh. Maybe there was nothing here. Or maybe there would be no great spark in the first moments but they would work up to falling in love. If they did.

Of course they would. Miranda Mack had predicted it.

Edmund stopped in front of Sarah and extended his hand. "The longer version. My name is Edmund Ford. I'm a widower of five years. This is my son, Carson, who you've met, of course. And my grandson, Danny, is asleep upstairs. I'm a banker at Texas Trust, where I've spent the past thirty years. About two months ago, I went to Madam Miranda to have my fortune told. She said my second great love was a green-eyed hairstylist named Sarah. She said I would know her right away, but that she had a small tattoo of a brush and blow-dryer on her ankle. I've been looking for her ever since. And now here she stands before me."

Sarah hadn't taken her gaze off Edmund, either. She lifted her chin as he clasped both his hands over hers.

"I understand from Carson that you're not comfortable with or particularly interested in your sister's prediction," Edmund continued. "So I'd like us to just forget that and have a nice dinner, welcoming you back into your niece's life. That's what this dinner will be. A welcome home celebration. Nothing more."

Olivia could tell her aunt liked that; Sarah's shoulders relaxed and she accepted a glass of wine from Edmund. They all sat down, Sarah and Edmund across from each other on the two couches, Olivia and Carson beside each other on the facing love seat.

They spent the next ten minutes making small talk about Tuckerville, Oak Creek, Blue Gulch, the rodeo, hairstyles, toddlers and Hurley's food truck. But it was very clear to Olivia that her aunt could not take her eyes off Edmund Ford. And the same went for Edmund.

Carson excused himself to the kitchen to check on dinner, and Olivia popped up to help.

"Olivia," Sarah said, worry in her eyes as she sat up very straight, staring at her niece.

"What's wrong?" Edmund asked, looking from Sarah to Olivia and back again.

"Please tell me the truth, Olivia," Sarah said. "Did you make dinner? Did you help?"

Ah. Olivia knew what her aunt was asking. She was worried that Olivia had infused dinner with amorous vibes. She hadn't cooked, helped or even stepped foot in the kitchen tonight.

"I promise you that I did not," Olivia said.

Sarah nodded. "Okay. Sorry for being so anxious."

"I must be missing something," Edmund said, confusion in his expression.

Olivia explained about her gift in as few words as possible so as not to make her aunt uncomfortable—and requested that Edmund keep it a secret. "I've never been all that comfortable with it myself, but I've come to accept that I do seem able to mend spirits with my cooking. At the least, I seem able to affect people positively."

Edmund grinned. "Well, no wonder you have lines for the food truck every day. Aside from the delicious po'boys. Who can't use a boost?"

"You feel differently about special abilities than your son does," Sarah said to Edmund.

"I've always been a realist," Edmund said. "But my mind and heart are open. I think that's the key to life."

Sarah bit her lip and sipped her wine but didn't respond.

"Well, I'll just go help Carson," Olivia said.

In the kitchen, Olivia practically slumped over at the counter. "I didn't even realize until this moment that I needed to come up for air."

Carson smiled as he slid the pasta carbonara, which looked and smelled amazing, into a serving dish. "You okay? I had the same reaction when I came in."

"I can't tell if there's anything between them," Olivia said. "I can see that they can't stop looking at each other, but no one's flirting or giving anything away."

Carson kneeled to peer into the oven, then shut it off and took out the garlic bread. "I know. My dad wears his heart on his sleeve these days but I'm not getting anything. Not a sign."

He wasn't gloating. He wasn't even smiling. Olivia took a knife and cut the garlic bread into pieces. "Could my mother have been wrong? I can't even imagine it."

Maybe her aunt didn't feel anything for Edmund Ford and vice versa. Maybe her mother *had* been wrong—this time. Maybe Carson had been right all along and this was some kind of a ruse for Edmund Ford to use his time and resources to find Aunt Sarah and bring her back to Blue Gulch for Olivia's sake?

No. Olivia just couldn't see her mother doing that.

"Dinnertime," Carson said, picking up the pasta and heading for the door. "Who knows, Olivia. They're both being so cagey. Maybe they'll announce their engagement by the first bite."

Olivia smiled. Carson sure had changed his tune.

By the time Carson was ready to serve dessert, chocolate-almond gelato, he still couldn't tell if there was anything between his father and Sarah Mack, but he knew the woman felt comfortable around Edmund because she'd opened up about her new willingness to look for the twins she'd given up for adoption, five years after her sister had told her that one of them had begun the process to find her. His dad had listened intently, asked questions without being too personal, and offered to help in any way he could.

"Dad, help me get dessert, will you?" Carson said.

His father excused himself and they headed into the kitchen.

"I have to say I'm almost a little let down," Carson said as he pulled out the gelato from the freezer. "Based on Olivia and Sarah insisting that Madam Miranda was the real deal, I was expecting firecrackers to be exploding across the ceiling, but I guess Miranda had it wrong."

Edmund peered through the archway, then leaned close to Carson. "Are you kidding? Madam Miranda was anything but wrong. I'm completely crazy about that woman."

Carson stared at his father, seeing the far-off dreaminess in the man eyes. "What? You haven't been acting like you're madly in love."

"For Sarah's sake. I know she's not looking for love. I know she's skittish and has a lot on her mind. And I know she's probably fighting what she may feel—if anything. I don't want to scare her out of my life."

"So what does it feel like?" Carson asked. "Attraction? Intrigue? Interest?"

"Much more than that," Edmund said. "It feels like I just met the woman I'm going to marry."

"Really?"

Edmund nodded. "Trust me, I was expecting to feel like I did back in high school, a wild crush, that kind of thing. But the feeling that swept over me when I laid eyes on Sarah Mack for the first time, and as I've gotten to know her a bit over the past hour, it's like I've known her my entire life. It's a depth of feeling I can't explain, Carson. But it looks like it's one-sided."

"But you're her great love, Dad. I'm sure she feels the same way—she's just fighting it like I told you she said she would."

Edmund shook his head. "I'm not so sure. Madam Miranda said that Sarah was *my* second great love. That doesn't mean I'm *hers*. You can be madly in love with someone who doesn't love you back. Isn't that the basis of most love songs?"

Carson had thought of that last night when he'd been talking to Sarah in front of her home. But hadn't Sarah said the fortune worked both ways?

And that she'd fight it?

Dammit. Had he gone through all this only to finally come around and then deliver the woman straight into father's arms when she'd break his heart, after all?

"She's just stunning," Edmund was saying in a dreamy tone, staring at the wall. "Those green eyes. And her voice. So melodic. She has such a fierce intellect, too. And despite the complicated quest she'll be embarking on, her sense of humor shines through. What a woman."

Carson stared at his father. Good grief. The man *was* in love. After fifty minutes.

"I miss her just being in here," Edmund whispered.

Whoa, boy.

"So, Aunt Sarah," Olivia asked as Carson and Edmund were busy in the kitchen. "Was Mom wrong? You don't seem to be very taken with Edmund."

"Are you kidding?" Sarah whispered. "I'm fighting my attraction to that amazing man with every fiber of my being. He's so handsome! And kind. There's such complexity to him. And the way he talks about his grandson is so sweet. Did you notice he has one dimple?"

Olivia laughed. "Yes. His son has the same. The grandson, too."

"But," Sarah said, her smile fading, "I'm not here for romance. The timing just isn't right. I want to find the twins, Olivia, and I don't know how I'm going to feel when I do. It's been so long since I allowed myself to think about those babies. And suddenly I'm going to meet them? I might not be able to handle it."

"You've been so strong, Sarah," Olivia said. "You'll be able to handle it. I'll be with you every step of the way, if you'll let me."

Sarah took her hand. "I'd like that. It means so much to me that you'd support me after I abandoned you the way I did. I wasn't even there for you when you lost your mother." Tears glistened in Sarah's eyes.

"I understand what happened, Sarah. I know how sometimes blocks can keep people away, how fear can grow and become a wall. But you're here. You're back. That's all that matters to me—the present and future."

Sarah leaned over and hugged Olivia. "Thank you."

"I understand what you mean about not wanting to acknowledge how you feel about Edmund," Olivia said. "But to push love away? Especially when you need it the most?"

"One thing at a time," Sarah said. "I've fought my feelings for the past thirty-two years. Literally repressed them. I'm a master at it, unfortunately. I can fight my feelings for a man I just met."

"Your predicted great love," Olivia clarified with a smile. "That's a little different than 'a man you just met.'"

Carson and Edmund came back into the dining room just then, Carson holding a tray with four fancy dishes of gelato. Olivia wondered at the conversation the two Ford men had had in the kitchen. If her aunt was smitten with Edmund, he must be smitten with her. He was very likely keeping himself in check so he wouldn't send Sarah running for the hills. Smart man.

After dessert and coffee, Carson said that he would start the process of finding the twins tomorrow morning.

Sarah nodded and stood up. "It's been quite a day and evening. I think I'll head home."

"I'd love it if you stayed with me," Olivia said. "Carson may need you in the morning to verify information or look at records."

"I'd like that," Sarah said.

As Olivia and her aunt headed to the door, the Ford men followed.

Sarah thanked Carson for dinner, and then told Edmund how nice it was to meet him. Olivia had the overpowering desire to stay, to convince her aunt to stay and linger with these two men they both clearly wanted to be with.

But her time with Carson was coming to an end. Had come an end, really. He'd done what he said he was going to do.

"Thank you," Olivia whispered to Carson, fighting the urge to lift her hand to his cheek, to kiss him.

And then she and her aunt were out the door, heading down the bluestone path to their cars in the driveway.

As they reached Sarah's car, her aunt said, "Tomorrow morning may change my entire life. Even the thought of having the twins' contact information scares me. I'm so damned afraid of not knowing what to expect." She shook her head. "Isn't *that* ironic. I suddenly wish I had a crystal ball."

Olivia squeezed her aunt's hand. "We'll face tomorrow together. You and me."

Sarah squeezed back. "Looks like there's already a 'you and me' where you're concerned," she said, upping her chin at the door, where Carson and Edmund both stood, watching them approach their cars. "You love that man. I know you do. I know it without having a shred of special ability."

She did love him. And it was *her* heart that was going to get broken in all this.

Chapter Thirteen

At one thirty in the afternoon the next day, Carson and Olivia waited in the reception area of Adoption Connections in Houston, the agency that had handled the twins' case. Carson had called first thing that morning to make an appointment for Sarah, and she'd been behind closed doors with the assistant director for almost a half hour.

"How does it work?" Olivia asked Carson, staring down the hallway. The pale yellow walls were lined with photographs of babies and children of all ages and races and shapes and sizes. "Will my aunt receive the names and addresses of the twins?"

Carson glanced at Olivia, who sat fidgeting beside him on the padded chair. He picked up her hand and held it for a moment. "The assistant director told me over the phone that once a clear match was made between adoptee and birth parent, that both would receive the contact information left by the other. So Sarah should receive a name and telephone number at the very least of the twin who initiated contract. Maybe at this point, both twins did."

"I wish I knew what was going on in there," Olivia said, straining her neck to see down the hall. "I wish we could have gone in there with her, but I understand that she wanted to talk to the assistant director alone."

Full circle, Sarah had said. She knew she had the support of Carson and her niece, but she wanted to be strong and come full circle. Carson felt for her as she'd walked down the hall alone. He'd wanted to stand up and tell her that she didn't have to be so tough, that she did have their support—and the support of a great man waiting for her in Blue Gulch, if only she'd open up her heart.

But who was he to talk about opening hearts?

The drive up to Houston had been tense, to say the least. Carson had picked up Sarah and Olivia at nine that morning, with coffee and muffins, but both women had been too nervous to partake. Sarah had mostly looked out the window. He'd been so aware of Olivia in the seat next to him. She wore a denim skirt and a pale pink blazer, her hair in a low ponytail like her aunt's. He'd held her hand throughout most of the long drive, and the fact that she'd let him was more startling than the realization that he cared that much about her. He knew he did, but every time he caught a glimpse of their hands intertwined, a strange chill would run up his spine, then settle, then sneak up again. Still, he'd left his hand where it was.

"I think I hear a door opening," Olivia said, standing up.

Carson stood, too, as footsteps came from down the hall. He could hear Sarah thanking the assistant director, and finally, she appeared, clutching a document and an envelope. She looked a bit stressed, but hopeful at the same time.

"Only one of the twins had initiated contact," Sarah said. "He left this letter for the file," she added, looking at it and biting her lip. She handed the envelope to Carson. "Will you read the letter, Carson?"

He nodded and they sat back down, Carson between the two women. He opened the envelope and took out a piece of white paper and began reading.

"I can't address this letter since I don't know your name or what to call you. Dear Birth Mother sounds too cold. I've often thought about you, but ever since I discovered I have a twin brother I never knew existed, I've decided to try to make contact. Please write back, email or call.
"Jake Morrow
"Black Bear Ranch
"RR 8
"Mill Valley, Texas"

"Jake Morrow," Sarah repeated, tears in her eyes.

It was dated five years earlier and included a telephone number and email address. Carson handed the letter to Sarah, who read it herself, then put it back inside the envelope.

"Jake Morrow. It's a nice name," Olivia said. "You okay, Aunt Sarah?"

Sarah twisted her lips. "Right before I gave birth I asked one of the nurses if the twins were going to be adopted together but I was told that was classified. Now I know they weren't."

"Do you think this is what my mother knew?" Olivia asked Sarah. "That one of the twins was trying to find the other?"

"Probably," Sarah said. "I'd like to help him do that, but I'm not sure how I can."

Carson had a feeling that Sarah wasn't ready to pick up the phone herself. "Mill Valley is just a couple of hours from Blue Gulch County," he said. "I could call Jake and arrange a meeting, if you'd like."

"I appreciate that. Although I'm not sure how much I can help with locating his twin."

"I can get started on that," Carson said. "Plus, even though the twins were adopted separately, Jake may have more information that he realizes. Parents, grandparents, old records, attics—you never know what you'll find or what's right in your house."

"In a matter of days I might actually be in contact with one of those tiny babies," Sarah said, her expression a combination of hope and wistfulness. "I almost can't believe it. My mother insisted it was for the best that I put it behind me and never speak of it. I wonder if she was trying to protect me by doing that, by acting as though none of it ever happened."

"But it did happen," Olivia said gently.

Sarah nodded and squeezed her niece's hand. "Yes, it most certainly did. And as strange as it feels to suddenly have it be the focus of my life, it feels good, too. And right. If I could know that the twins are okay, I would be at peace."

Olivia slung her arm around her aunt. "Well, we're here for you, Sarah. You know that right?"

Sarah nodded. "Thank you, both. From the bottom of my heart." She stood up. "Let's head home."

Carson noticed that Sarah kept the letter from Jake in her hand instead of putting it in her purse. She felt a connection to him and was letting herself feel it, which was good. She wasn't shutting down or off. Carson had a good feeling about all this.

Finally, three hours later, they arrived back at Olivia's house, a huge bouquet of wildflowers waiting in a round basket on the porch. Olivia plucked the card. It was addressed to Sarah.

"For me?" Sarah asked, taking the card. She read.

Dear Sarah,
    I hope today went well. I recall you said last night at dinner that wildflowers always made you feel better. If you could use an ear or a distraction, I'm available. 555-2345
Yours,
Edmund Ford

Sarah breathed in the colorful bouquet, a soft smile on her face. "That was thoughtful and very kind. I'll call to thank him." At the door, she turned to Carson. "Thank you again for everything."

"My pleasure," Carson said, watching Sarah head inside.

Olivia wasn't surprised at his father's gesture. That was his dad.

"Come in for a cup of coffee?" Olivia asked on the porch. She knew he probably wanted to get home to

Danny, but she wanted to prolong his leaving for just five more minutes.

"I should get home," he said. "But after six hours in the car today, I could use a strong cup of coffee."

Good, she thought. *Me, too.* In the kitchen, Olivia lifted an ear toward the doorway and smiled. "I still hear her talking," she whispered to Carson. "Maybe she's loosening up on her stronghold against love."

"I hope so." If anyone needed love in her life, Olivia thought, it was Sarah Mack.

"Now she's laughing," Olivia said. "That's nice to hear."

Carson nodded. "A huge weight was lifted off her chest. She did something she's probably been thinking about, fretting over for five years. All that had been blocking her before may naturally lift away. She may be readier for a relationship than she realizes."

And you? she wanted to ask. *You are, too, and just don't know it.*

Or was that wishful thinking?

Her aunt acted and was getting results. She was taking charge, doing something. It was time for Olivia to do the same. She loved this man and she was going to show him. She was going to ask for what she wanted. *Him.*

She slid her arms around Carson's neck and kissed him, backing him against the counter.

At first, he responded, deepening the kiss, his hand weaving in her hair, down her back, his other hand sliding up her tank top toward her bra. Every nerve ending was on delicious fire. She pressed herself against him, her hands against his muscular chest, never wanting this moment to end. Carson, Carson, Carson.

But the moment did end.

He slowly pulled away, shaking his head. "I want you so bad, Olivia. You have no idea. But—" He stepped farther away, straightening his shirt, his expression...wary, and her heart crumbled.

She turned her face away so that he wouldn't see how disappointed she was. She moved to the coffeemaker, pretending great interest in lining up the creamer and sugar bowl. *But I don't love you and don't want to hurt you.* She had no doubt that was the rest of the sentence.

"I—" he began, but said nothing else.

Oh, hell. "I appreciate what you're doing for my aunt," she said, trying to keep her voice even. "She'll keep me informed about Jake and your progress locating the other twin, so..."

So... Don't leave, she wanted to scream. *Stop me from trying to save face and make this less uncomfortable for you. Tell me you love me and I'm worth blasting through your wall for.*

She could feel him staring at her, and she glanced at him, his hazel-green eyes flashing with an intensity. She thought he might say something, but he just nodded and left.

From down the hall, she could hear her aunt telling Edmund Ford a funny story about the time she colored her own hair a bright orange. The sound of her aunt's light laughter was like a soothing balm against her own crumbling heart.

Carson had spent a restless night tossing and turning and thinking about Olivia, about the expression on her beautiful face when he'd walked out last night. Didn't she know how badly he wanted her? That he loved her but couldn't face it and so would rather just ignore his feelings by not acting on them.

Like her aunt was. Who he knew was making a huge mistake by doing so.

Why was his life not making sense? This was nuts. Why could he see it for Sarah and not himself.

Because she's not you, dummy, he told himself. It's easy to think this or that about someone else and a lot harder to practice what you preach.

And while he'd been calling himself a fool for knowing what was what and still refusing to do anything about it—such as go get his woman and tell her he was a dope and that he loved her and wanted to spend his life with her—he'd stayed put on his couch. Not doing any of the above. Paralyzed with… "I can't-itis." Then his father had kept him on the phone for an hour, sounding like a dreamy romantic who couldn't stop talking about the woman he loved. Apparently, Edmund and Sarah had spent almost two hours on the phone, talking about everything. His father sounded so happy, so lighthearted, so hopeful that his second great love was going to open her heart to him, after all, that Carson had almost called Olivia and asked her to come over since Danny was sleeping.

But the thought of Danny stopped him in his tracks again. Danny. Left by his mother. Now here Carson was, about to open his life and home and heart to another woman. He'd trusted the first time around, thought he'd had everything he wanted, thought his family would be forever.

But it wasn't.

For himself, for Danny, he'd stay a lone wolf.

Now, he sat in his home office, taking another sip of the very strong coffee he'd made and watched the clock finally hit 9:00 a.m, a reasonable time to make telephone calls.

He picked up his cell phone and pressed in the number Jake Morrow had left in the letter. Carson had easily found his home telephone number, as well.

A deep voice answered. "Hello."

"Jake Morrow?" Carson asked.

"Speaking."

"My name is Carson Ford. I'm a private investigator in Blue Gulch County. Your birth mother, Sarah Mack, asked me to contact you. Via Adoption Connections of Houston, she received the letter you sent five years ago about your interest in finding your biological twin brother. She'd like to meet you and help locate him, if she can."

Jake Morrow was silent for a moment. "I appreciate the call," he said. "But that was five years ago. A lot's happened in that time. I'm no longer interested in contact with either my birth mother or my twin brother. Thanks for calling, though. Goodbye."

Click.

Oh, dammit.

Though she wasn't due at Hurley's Homestyle Kitchen food truck until eleven thirty, Olivia headed over at nine thirty, needing to get out of the house, plus she wanted to give Sarah some privacy. She heard her talking to Edmund on the telephone again this morning. There was flirtation. Laughter. Happiness. Olivia's heart had leaped for her aunt, but she herself was down in the dumps this morning. She'd had a horrible night's sleep, unable to get comfortable, waking up and thinking about a certain sexy private investigator who was acting like his own worst enemy.

Unless he just didn't return her feelings. Maybe she was giving herself too much credit, thinking he loved her deep down when he didn't.

But she knew he loved her. She felt it every time he looked at her. It was in how he spoke to her, his expression, the way he brought her coffee just the way she liked it, how he'd helped her aunt, driving all the way to Houston and back. The man loved her!

Right?

She'd moped for a good five minutes, then had gone into her mother's fortune-telling parlor, hoping to soak up some truths in the air, but all she felt was her own truth—that *she* loved Carson.

She was almost at the food truck when her cell phone rang.

Carson. "I spoke to Jake Morrow this morning. He said he changed his mind about making contact with his birth mother or twin brother and hung up."

She stopped in her tracks. Oh, no. "Carson, now what? That'll break Aunt Sarah's heart."

"Let's talk it through. Can you stop by this morning? I've got Danny with me."

So she could break her own heart even more? "I'll be right there."

She headed back home and got in her car and drove over to Carson's. He and Danny were waiting for her on the porch, Danny holding his yellow monkey in one hand and a cheese stick in the other.

"Hi, Liva!" Danny said.

She tapped his nose. "Hey, sweetie."

"Come on in," Carson said. "Danny, want to build Olivia a tower of blocks?"

"Yes!" Danny said and went running for his play area in the family room.

Olivia followed Carson into the kitchen, sending Danny a smile as he worked on his tower. He handed her a mug of coffee—just the way she liked it, of course.

He sipped his own coffee as they headed into the family room and sat down on the plush sofa. "I think your aunt should write Jake Morrow a letter and send it to his home. Explain herself, in her own words, anything she'd like to say. At least she'll be a real person rather than an idea in Jake's mind. What do think?"

"It's a good idea. Plus, it'll give her something proactive to do. It's been five years since Jake sent that letter—with no contact from his birth mother. I think Sarah will understand that he might have been put off by that. I'll talk to her."

Carson's cell phone rang. "Maybe Jake Morrow calling back? Changed his mind, perhaps."

Hope blossomed in Olivia's chest. "You answer your calls. I'll play with Danny."

Carson headed into his office to answer the phone, and Olivia went to Danny's play area.

Danny stood in front of his tower of big blocks, almost as high as he was. "Meatball," he said, giggling and pointing at the top block.

"To put on top? All covered with cheese?" Olivia said, ticking the little goofball.

Danny laughed. "Top 'getti," he sang, then doubled over in laughter.

Olivia scooped up Danny into a hug, smelling his

baby shampoo–scented head. She never wanted to let him go.

She loved this little boy. And she loved the man down the hall.

And she was going to fight for them.

"Danny, I'm going to put you in your playpen for a few minutes with your talking panda while I talk to your daddy, okay?"

He rubbed his eyes and yawned. "'Kay."

She picked up the sleepyhead and set him down in the playpen, giving him a kiss on the head, then marched into Carson's office and shut the door.

"Was that Jake?" she asked.

"No. It was actually Joey Johnson letting me know his dad came to his Little League practice this morning and then took him out for breakfast and he had a great time."

"Aww," Olivia said. "I'm very glad." She cleared her throat. "Danny's in his playpen. I'm going to head home to talk to Sarah about writing that letter to Jacob. But before I go, I want to tell you something."

He stared at her. "Okay," he said, as though bracing himself. He stood up from his desk chair and leaned against the window.

"I want to speak my mind, Carson, because if I don't, I'll always wonder if telling you would have made a difference."

"Tell me what?" he asked.

Do it. Tell him. She sucked in a deep breath. "That I love you. That I'm in love with you. I love you and I love Danny and I want us all to have a future."

He was quiet for a moment, then said, "Olivia. I…

trusted in love once and it blew up on me. I can't do this again. I'm very sorry."

Not good enough, buster, sorry. She squared her shoulders and lifted her chin. "And if you'd gone to see Madam Miranda and she told you I was your second great love? Then what?"

"Olivia. I never would have gone to see your mother for a reading of my fortune, so it's a moot point."

"But if you had. If she'd told you."

"That we were destined for each other?" he asked. She nodded.

"I don't believe in that, Olivia. Reality is Jake Morrow hanging up in my ear. That's life. There's no guarantees about anything."

"Carson," she said.

"I think your aunt should write that letter," he said, his tone making clear he was done with the conversation.

No. He was not dismissing her again. She knew this man loved her. She knew it in her heart, mind and soul. "Carson—"

He moved away from the window and came around the desk until he was standing just inches from her. "I wouldn't need a crystal ball to tell me that we belong together, Olivia. I already know it. I feel it in every cell of my body. I feel it running through my veins. I feel it here all the time," he said, pressing his hand over his heart.

She gasped. "But—"

"But I'm fighting it. I've been fighting it and I'll keep fighting it. So that Danny and I never have to go through that kind of pain again. Weren't you the one who said, Olivia, that people do all kinds of things even when they know the truth? You could be madly in love with me and destined to be with me and—"

He stopped and turned away.

"And what, Carson?" she asked gently.

"And I could lose you anyway. Destiny gives, destiny takes."

"Carson, the only thing I can guarantee you is that I love you and your little boy with all my heart. But, yeah, life can pull some fast ones. I'd like you to be by my side when they happen."

"Liva? Daddy?" a little voice said through the closed door.

"Danny's calling," he said, heading to the door. He seemed very relieved by the interruption. "I'm sorry, Olivia," he added, turning to face her for a moment. He tilted his head. "I really am sorry. Let me know when your aunt sends the letter."

Dammit, he was frustrating. How the hell was she going to get through to this man?

Chapter Fourteen

An entire week had passed since Carson had seen Olivia. He'd taken on two new cases, a complicated one for the Oak Creek police department involving a potential burglary suspect who'd skipped town, and the other for a middle-aged high school English teacher convinced that her husband was cheating on her, but wanted some kind of proof before she "did anything reckless." Carson had always avoided the spying-on-spouses jobs, but he was in a bad mood this week and the client had caught him on his worst day, so he'd taken the case.

Yesterday he'd trailed the husband to an Italian restaurant in Tuckerville, where the fiftysomething man met a young woman who spent the next forty-five minutes giving him Italian lessons. Then he followed the man to a bookstore, where he purchased two travel guides to Rome and a birthday card with a cover that read "For my beautiful wife." When the man took the card over to the little café area, Carson ordered a coffee and sat at the table beside him, glancing over as the man wrote inside the card—"My beloved Carla" and a bunch of romantic stuff—then put in what looked like boarding passes for an airline flight. Considering that Carson's client's name was Carla, Carson had figured he could call it a day. He'd called his client right away to inform her that he was one hundred percent sure her husband was not cheating. That night, the client texted him that Carson was right; her husband had just surprised her with a trip to Italy and even knew how to say a bunch of Italian phrases.

The whole thing had given Carson a headache. He hadn't been expecting the case to turn out that way. Score one for love and marriage. Carson: zero.

His doorbell rang and for a moment his heart sped up when he thought it might be Olivia, but he'd done such a great job of pushing her away that he was sure it wasn't her. Dammit, he missed her. The sight of her pretty face and crazy skirts and the sound of her voice and how soft her lips always looked, and the way she turned his head around, made him want to join the world instead of staying behind lock and key. But a week later, he'd stayed where he was, working, stewing, taking care of Danny and watching his father fall more and more deeply in love with Sarah Mack.

Though Sarah still insisted she wasn't looking to get involved in a romance, she and Edmund had gotten together every day since the return from the adoption agency. Edmund had seen her through the first couple of days of heartache when Olivia had let her aunt know that Jake Morrow had changed his mind about contact. And Edmund had been there when she was ready to start writing the letter to Jake. According to his father, Sarah had spent days working on the letter, thinking about it, deleting it, rewriting it; and she and Edmund had taken long walks into the woods, Edmund silent by her side so she could think, his father simply a source of support, of friendship.

Last night, his father had called him at midnight to report that he'd asked Sarah if he could kiss her good-night after their date, and she'd finally said yes, and all the fireworks and clanging cymbals had made their noise. Edmund Ford was deeply in love.

Even if she breaks my heart, it was worth just feeling the way I do right now, his dad had said.

The fortune had come true. His father had found his predicted second great love and destiny had taken its course. How else could Carson look at it? Yesterday, he'd tried falling back on his preferred power-of-suggestion explanation. His dad had been told he'd feel a certain way about a certain someone, Sarah had made it all the more stakes worthy by being truly "hard to get," and his dad had fallen hard.

Except that didn't sound or feel right to Carson, either. What had happened between Edmund and Sarah was very real. And, yes, Carson had to admit, beautiful.

He still didn't believe in the whole fortune thing, well, not completely, but it was staring him in the face every time he looked at his father, every time his father talked about Sarah. All Carson really knew for sure was that he was happy for his dad. Edmund Ford deserved all the love and happiness in the world.

Carson opened the door to find the man himself standing on the porch, holding an envelope.

"Sarah finally wrote the letter to Jake," Edmund said. "She thought you might like to read it."

Carson raised an eyebrow. "That's all right. I'm sure it's deeply personal."

"Sarah wants to make sure you think she handled it just right," his dad said. "You've been there with her throughout and have experience with hitting the right notes so that someone you're seeking doesn't run away. Drop it off at the post office when you're done, will you?"

Edmund held out the letter, and Carson finally took it. "Give Danny a hug for me," his father added as he headed to his car. "Remind him that Sarah and I are taking him to the town carnival at four."

Carson nodded and watched his father walk away, the old skip in his step. The man exuded happiness. Honestly, he didn't know how his dad could take it, handle it, deal with such a tentative relationship when he felt so strongly about Sarah. The woman was a bit fragile and could bolt at any time. She'd basically said as much from the get-go and, according to Edmund, reiterated that every day. And still, his father acted like all was well. Carson could never deal with that kind of uncertainty.

Uncertainty. Huh. It struck him how ironic that was. If only he could be sure that Olivia wouldn't pull a fast one on him and Danny… Despite a complete lack of evidence that she ever would. Despite her telling him that she loved him. Was in love with him. Loved Danny. He still couldn't…let go enough to let her in.

He closed the door and walked upstairs to Danny's nursery to check on him. His son was sound asleep in his crib, clutching his yellow monkey. Carson went back downstairs to his office and sat behind his desk, wanting to read Sarah's letter in an official capacity instead of a personal one. He was her PI, after all. This was business. Even if she was his father's great love. And the aunt of the woman he refused to allow himself to love.

He slid the letter from the unsealed envelope. It was handwritten in black ink.

Dear Jake,

My name is Sarah Mack. When I was sixteen years old, I gave birth to fraternal twin boys on February 15, thirty-two years ago. I never saw you or your twin, I never had the opportunity to hold you. And although I tried very hard not to think of you both over the years in order to protect my heart, I thought about the two of you every day.

If you would like to meet, to ask questions, for closure, for anything I may able to tell you so that you can locate your twin, I would be happy to do that. I apologize for not availing myself to the registry five years ago when you first sought me out. I wasn't ready then. But I am ready now.

One thing I've learned lately is that holding yourself back from your own happiness and well-being, especially because of fear or anger, hurts others just as much as it hurts ourselves.

Your birth mother, Sarah Mack.

It was a good letter, just right, Carson thought. But instead of putting it in the envelope and sealing it up to mail, he kept staring at that last line. *Hurts others just as much as it hurts ourselves...*

He hadn't wanted to hurt Olivia.

And not only had he hurt her, but he'd also hurt Danny, who asked for "Liva" and the spaghetti song every day.

Joey Johnson's tear-streaked face came to mind, the boy sitting in his car, scared to death over confronting his dad, with no idea if his father would reject him. Then Carson's own dad's words floated through his head. *Even if she breaks my heart, it was worth just feeling the way I do right now.*

But Carson didn't want to feel the way *he* did right now: alone, heavyhearted, with one sixteenth of the bravery of his nine-year-old client. Even Sarah had come around by saying yes to a good-night kiss—choosing love over fear.

Carson sealed the envelope and when Danny's sitter arrived, he headed out. He had a very important letter to mail. And then a very important errand to run. And finally, a very important woman to see.

Olivia handed her teary-eyed customer the tuna-melt po'boy with extra cucumbers that she'd ordered, and watched the woman sit down at a table. She took a bite. Then another. The another. She lifted her chin. Then ate another bite. She bit her lip, pulled out her phone and pressed in a number, then had a conversation Olivia couldn't hear.

Suddenly, a guy came running down the street toward the food truck. The young woman stood and went running toward him like in a slow-motion TV commercial. The two embraced and walked off, hand in hand.

Ah, Olivia thought with a smile. A rueful smile, though, these days. *If only my own ability worked on me. Or Carson.* She wouldn't want Carson to come into her life via any kind of magic other than the natural kind, but a little head start? She'd take it. A head start for Carson would come in the form of a tiny pickax to knock away at the armor.

As Olivia prepared today's special po'boy, a good old-fashioned Italian, she noticed the three Hurley sisters coming up to the window. With them was a pretty brunette she didn't recognize.

"Hi, Olivia!" Georgia called out, flipping her shiny brown hair behind her shoulders. Georgia was the eldest and baked for Hurley's Homestyle Kitchen.

"Got a second?" Annabel, the middle sister, asked. "We'd like to introduce you to our cousin and new part-time cook, Emma Hurley."

Emma smiled and held up a hand at Olivia.

"Emma here is not only a whiz in the kitchen, but she's proving herself to be a great baker, too," Clementine, the youngest and a waitress, said.

Georgia nodded. "Yesterday Emma helped me make six apple pies—I was told they had the best crust ever." Since Georgia was the baker for the restaurant, that was high praise. Olivia always loved how warm and welcoming and kind the Hurley sisters were; they never looked at people as competition, worrying that Olivia would start her own food truck and leave them in the lurch, or that great baker Emma would steal thunder from Georgia. Olivia owed the Hurleys a lot. She'd never forget how they'd given her a fresh start when she'd needed one. Olivia had come to really love the Hurley's Homestyle Kitchen food truck.

She came outside, the warm, breezy March air refreshing.

Emma extended her hand toward Olivia. "I really appreciate the job at Hurley's Homestyle Kitchen. I'm new in town."

Olivia shook the woman's hand. Emma looked to be in her midtwenties with big blue eyes and soft, wavy golden-brown hair to her shoulders...and a secret, Olivia sensed. She had a good feeling about Emma, though.

"Emma's mostly going to be working at the restaurant," Annabel said, "but we thought she could learn the ropes of the truck so that she could help out during rushes or pinch-hit if you or Dylan are sick. I know your busy time is about to start, Olivia, so could you use a hand?"

"I'd love the help," Olivia said, smiling at Emma.

Fifteen minutes later, Olivia had just finished giving Emma the lay of the land and going over the recipes for all the po'boys and cannoli when a crowd came out of Texas Trust and headed for the food truck. Then the real estate office crew walked over.

Olivia gestured with her chin at the people coming their way. "We're about to get as busy as Annabel said."

"I'm ready!" Emma said, rolling up her sleeves.

Olivia smiled. Emma might have a secret up those sleeves, but she liked her and was grateful for her very competent help.

By the end of the lunch rush—almost two hundred po'boys and over a hundred cannoli—Olivia could finally sit down at the little desk by the driver's seat and clink a lemonade toast with Emma to a rush gone well. As she made a mini strawberry cannoli for Emma,

Olivia was struck by the notion that Emma Hurley had a big secret to share with someone—someone she was having trouble finding.

She tried to ask her new assistant a few questions about herself, but Emma was a bit cagey and Olivia realized that the woman probably didn't want to be asked questions. Emma helped clean up like a champ and then Olivia said she might as well clock out for the day.

A shadow loomed at the window and at first Olivia thought Emma was back, but it was Carson.

Her heart moved. He looked so damned handsome. He wore a navy blue Henley shirt and sexy jeans and his brown cowboy boots. She hadn't laid eyes on him in an entire week, but she'd sensed she hadn't seen the last of Carson Ford. He needed time, to think and process and mull—and miss her. She didn't know how long that would take, but she was sure glad to see him now. It definitely meant the *missing* part had begun.

He took off his aviator sunglasses. "I'd love a shrimp po'boy."

She smiled. "That's what you ordered the day I met you."

"I'm trying for a do-over," he said. "I wasn't very nice to you that day. And that night, you told me about your gift when I was walking you home from my dad's house. I didn't believe you, even though I saw some evidence of it since. Like with that pushy lady."

"I remember," she said, reaching for the container of shrimp that Emma had helped her season. He was simply "making nice." Her aunt and his dad were an item, and it made sense for Carson to be on good, friendly terms with Olivia.

"If you do have a gift," he added, "I'd appreciate it

if you'd infuse my po'boy with a little assurance. A lot of assurance, actually."

She moved closer to the window. "Assurance for what?"

He disappeared from view and the door to the food truck opened. He stepped up inside. "That the woman I love will forgive me for being so stubborn."

A rush of happiness zinged from Olivia's toes to the top of her head.

"I love you, Olivia Mack. I love everything you are." He opened a little velvet box; a beautiful diamond ring sparkled. "The sales guy at Blue Gulch Jewelers told me this ring was destined for my bride. That was the exact word he used."

She laughed. "You don't believe in destiny."

"But I believe in how I feel about you. I'm just going to run with that. That's what I want to teach Danny. To love, to be open, not to run away. I *love* you, Olivia," he said.

"I love you, too."

He kissed her, then pulled back. "I wasn't sure about proposing here—if you'd want to remember that you got engaged in a food truck. But this is where we met, after all."

Happy tears poked at her eyes. "There's no place that could have been more special."

"I guess it was destiny," he said, kissing her again.

Epilogue

Four weeks later, on a breathtaking, warm and breezy late-March evening, Olivia stood with Dory Drummond in the beautiful backyard of Edmund Ford's mansion, admiring the twinkling white lights strung among the trees. Hundreds of guests at Edmund and Sarah's engagement party mingled, sipping champagne and trying appetizers that uniformed waiters appeared with on round silver trays.

"If I could have your attention," Edmund said, standing in front of the weeping willow and clinking his glass with a spoon. Aunt Sarah stood beside him, looking so lovely in her pale yellow dress and strappy sandals, her curly auburn hair down around her shoulders. "I'd like to thank you all for coming to share in my good fortune." He shot a wink at Carson, who was standing a few feet from Olivia with Beaufort Harrington. "Until very recently, I never thought I would find a second chance at happiness. But this wonderful woman changed all that. I'm very happy to announce that Sarah and I have set a wedding date for September and you're all invited."

There was a big round of applause and excited chatter as guests crowded around the happy couple. Olivia excused herself from Dory and rushed up to her aunt, wrapping her in a hug.

"When Edmund first proposed last week," Sarah said, "I was so flabbergasted, but my answer was in my heart. A very big and sure yes. My fiancé has been asking what kind of wedding I'd like, and I was thinking maybe we'd elope, but I don't want such a big and special day to pass without you there. Or Carson. You're both family."

"I wouldn't want to miss your wedding, Aunt Sarah," Olivia said, so thrilled for the woman. "Just think, by the fall we'll both be married women."

"I just might join that club, too," Dory said as she joined them, her expression all dreamy as she gazed at Beaufort. "What a difference a month makes. Now that Beau and I have gotten to know each other apart from any expectations, we're madly in love."

"I'm so happy for you, Dory," Olivia said, hugging her dear friend.

The huge Hurley group came over to meet Sarah, and Olivia made the introductions. There were Annabel and West, Georgia and Nick, Clementine and Logan, and even seventy-five-year-old Essie Hurley had a date, the charming and dapper owner of the independent bookstore on the far end of Blue Gulch Street. Love was most definitely in the air in Blue Gulch, Texas.

Sarah's cell phone rang, and she reached into her little sequined purse for it. "Unfamiliar number," she said. "Hello?" She listened for a moment, her left hand flying to her mouth. She looked like she might cry.

Oh, no. What was this? Olivia wondered.

Sarah turned and walked a few feet away, standing beside the weeping willow as if to talk in private. Wait, was she smiling now? Suddenly the hand was back at her mouth. She was pacing a bit, talking, then listening. Then smiling. Then just standing very still, staring out at the night.

Finally, she put the phone away and came over to Olivia. "Let's go find Carson and Edmund," Sarah said. "I have some news to share."

Wondering what was up, Olivia scanned the crowd. "There's Edmund. He's standing with Carson and a few others."

They walked over to find Edmund and Carson listening to one of the men telling a very long story about a Texas Trust deal; they both looked a little bored, so Olivia figured it was a good time to steal them away. She gestured them over.

The four of them walked across the yard and stood behind another tree.

"I just received a telephone call from Jake Morrow," Sarah said. "It's been a month since I wrote that letter to him, and I'd pretty much given up hope that he'd want contact. But he said he'd spent some time thinking things over and he would like to meet me."

"That's great!" Olivia said, squeezing her aunt's hand. "I'm so glad he responded." Over the past month, every day that the mail hadn't brought a letter and the phone hadn't rung with a call from Jake, Olivia had noticed a bit of sad wistfulness in the air around her aunt. But now, there was joy on her face.

Edmund wrapped his fiancée in a hug. "I'm so happy for you."

"I had a feeling he'd come around," Carson said. "Jake started the ball rolling five years ago, then stopped it, so the want—the need—was there. Is he coming to Blue Gulch or will you travel to his ranch?"

"He's coming to Blue Gulch next Saturday," Sarah said. "He said he'd like to see where he began, understand a little about his birth family. And he *is* hoping I can help him locate his twin brother. So far, he's had no luck with that."

"Well, I'll certainly help if I can," Carson said, his arm around Olivia.

Olivia noticed her aunt was looking at her as though wondering something, trying to figure out if Sarah should say what was on her mind.

"Sarah?" Olivia prompted.

"I was just thinking," she began, glancing at Edmund and Carson, and then back at Olivia. "Since we're both engaged to these wonderful men here, and they're family and we're family, wouldn't it be nice to have a double wedding?"

Olivia gasped. "I'd love it!"

"We're already each other's best man," Carson said, looking at his dad, "so that works."

Olivia smiled. "And Danny can be our ring bearer. I can just see him in his little tuxedo."

"Two dads down the aisle with our beautiful brides," Edmund said. "Count me in."

With the people she loved most beside her and the stars twinkling overhead, Olivia felt her mother's presence more strongly than she ever had these months without Miranda.

"Want to know something?" Carson whispered as the foursome began heading back to the party.

"What?" she asked, unable to drag her gaze away from Carson's handsome face, his hazel-green eyes.

"When I kissed Danny good-night before heading over to your house to pick you up, he said something I think you're going to like."

She couldn't imagine being any happier than she was right now. "What did he say?"

"He said, 'Liva mama?'"

Olivia's heart flip-flopped. "He did? He said that?"

Carson nodded and stopped on the grass, holding her close.

"I am going to be his mama," she whispered, her cup running over to the point that tears were threatening.

"I owe this all to a fortune, destiny, stubbornness, reality, life and hard work," Carson said. "All of that. It all played a part. I'm just glad it did."

She leaned up to kiss her fiancé. "Me, too. Because *love* played the biggest part of all."

* * * * *

Look for Jake Morrow and Emma Hurley's story, CHARM SCHOOL FOR COWBOYS, in May 2017 as the HURLEY'S HOMESTYLE KITCHEN *miniseries continues!*

COMING NEXT MONTH FROM

H HARLEQUIN®

SPECIAL EDITION

Available February 21, 2017

#2533 FORTUNE'S SECOND-CHANCE COWBOY
The Fortunes of Texas: The Secret Fortunes • by Marie Ferrarella
Young widow Chloe Fortune Eliot falls for Chance Howell, an ex-soldier with PTSD, but will their fear of another heartbreak stop them both from seizing a second chance at love?

#2534 JUST A LITTLE BIT MARRIED
The Bachelors of Blackwater Lake • by Teresa Southwick
Rose Tucker is a single woman with a failing business. Or so she thinks. Then her ex, Lincoln Hart, shows up with an offer for her design services...and the bombshell that a paperwork glitch makes them a little bit married.

#2535 KISS ME, SHERIFF!
The Men of Thunder Ridge • by Wendy Warren
Even as Willa Holmes vows not to risk loving again after a tragedy, she finds herself the subject of a hot pursuit by local sheriff Derek Neel. Can she escape the loving arm of the law? Does she even want to?

#2536 THE MARINE MAKES HIS MATCH
Camden Family Secrets • by Victoria Pade
Kinsey Madison has a strict policy about dating military men: she won't. Of course that means she can team up with Lieutenant Colonel Sutter Knightlinger to get his widowed mother settled and Kinsey in contact with her new family without risking her heart...right?

#2537 PREGNANT BY MR. WRONG
The McKinnels of Jewell Rock • by Rachael Johns
When anonymous advice columnist and playboy Quinn McKinnel receives a letter from Pregnant by Mr. Wrong, he recognizes the sender as Bailey Sawyer, his one-night-stand, and has to decide whether to simply fess up or win over the mother of his child.

#2538 A FAMILY UNDER THE STARS
Sugar Falls, Idaho • by Christy Jeffries
On a "glamping" trip for her magazine, Charlotte Folsom has a fling with her guide, Alex Russell. But back in Sugar Falls, they keep running into each other, and their respective families fill a void neither knew was missing. Will Charlotte and Alex be too stubborn to see the forest for the trees?

YOU CAN FIND MORE INFORMATION ON UPCOMING HARLEQUIN® TITLES, FREE EXCERPTS AND MORE AT WWW.HARLEQUIN.COM.

HSECNM0217

Chance knew he should just go. Normally, he would have.
But something was making him dig in his heels and stay.
He wanted to get something straight.

"Is this the kind of stuff you're going to be feeding
those boys?" he asked. "Stuff about slaying dragons?"

"No, this is the kind of 'stuff' I'm going to be using
in order to try to understand the boys," she said. "To help
them reconnect with the world."

He laughed drily. Still sounded like a bunch of mumbo
jumbo to him.

"Well, good luck with that," he told her, shaking
his head. "But if you ask me, a little hard work and a
little responsibility should help those boys do all the
reconnecting that they need."

"Hard work and responsibility," she repeated, as if he
had just quoted scripture. "Has it helped you?" Chloe
asked innocently.

His scowl deepened for a moment, and then he just

waved her words away. "Don't try getting inside my head, Chloe Elliott. There's nothing in it for you. I'm doing just fine just the way I am."

She suppressed a sigh. "Okay, as long as you're happy."

Happy? When was the last time he'd been happy? He couldn't remember.

"Happy's got nothing to do with it," Chance answered. "I'm my own man on my own terms, and that's all that really counts."

He felt himself losing his temper, and he didn't want to do that. Once things were said, they couldn't get unsaid, and a lot of damage could be done. He didn't want that to happen. Not with this woman.

"I'd better go find the boss. Graham said that he wanted to take me around the spread as soon as I stashed my gear."

She didn't want to be the reason he was late. "Then I guess you'd better get going."

"Yeah, I guess I'd better." With that, he crossed back to the door.

He walked out feeling that there were things left unspoken. A great many things. But then, maybe it was better that way. He wasn't looking to have his head "shrunk" any more than it already was. Even if the lady doing the shrinking was nothing short of a knockout.

Some things, he reasoned, were just better off left alone.

Don't miss
FORTUNE'S SECOND-CHANCE COWBOY
by Marie Ferrarella,
available March 2017 wherever
Harlequin® Special Edition books and ebooks are sold.

www.Harlequin.com

HSEEXP0217

#1 _New York Times_ bestselling author

SHERRYL WOODS

**introduces a sweet-talkin' man to shake
things up in Serenity.**

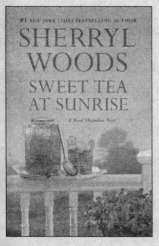

Emotionally wounded single
mom Sarah Price has come
home to Serenity, South
Carolina, for a fresh start. With
support from her two best
friends—the newest generation
of the Sweet Magnolias—she
can face any crisis.

But sometimes a woman
needs more than even treasured
friends can provide. Sexy
Travis McDonald may be
exactly what Sarah's battered
self-confidence requires. The
newcomer is intent on getting
Sarah to work at his fledgling
radio station…and maybe into
his bed, as well.

Sarah has learned not to trust sweet words. She'll measure the
man by his actions. Is Travis the one to heal her heart? Or will he
break it again?

Available now, wherever books are sold!

THE WORLD IS BETTER WITH

Romance

Harlequin has everything from contemporary, passionate and heartwarming to suspenseful and inspirational stories.

Whatever your mood, we have a romance just for you!

Connect with us to find your next great read, special offers and more.

f /HarlequinBooks

🐦 @HarlequinBooks

www.HarlequinBlog.com

www.Harlequin.com/Newsletters

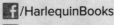

H HARLEQUIN®

A *Romance* FOR EVERY MOOD™

www.Harlequin.com